# Sculptor of Stories

RAY DACOLIAS

Sculptor of Stories

Copyright © 2015 by Ray Dacolias

ISBN 978-0-9895646-5-6

"Oblivion" is dedicated to my good friend, Russell, that bold and adventurous traveler, who one day suggested that we ought to visit that most enigmatic and fascinating of places, the Salton Sea.

# Contents

# The Fountain of Youth

In the House of Death, flesh becomes stone,
here it sleeps, in this manmade tomb;
the memories of yesterday, living in its fetid womb,
the end of the procession, buried in this weary gloom

Gilbert Gonzalez was calcified, he truly was, and he knew he was, as he had expected to turn into living stone and accept it, as his father had and his father's father had before him, as everyone around him had, too; thus, it was cultural wisdom that you are born strong and you get stronger and then you become weak and grow weaker until finally your decaying body is held together by sagging flesh and brittle bone and beige bandages. Gilbert knew it was coming as certain as the changing of the seasons and the turning of the earth, so once he arrived at the village of the condemned, he merely accepted it in the same manner you accept any inevitable event, by bowing deeply before it and capitulating to it and then settling down for what he hoped was a short stay in this stagnant pool of perdition. Yes, he mused, in his tiny bedroom chamber of the living dead, I have friends who come here but as much as I enjoy it, I abhor it, as I am somewhat embarrassed to be so inflicted with the ravages of old age that I have no energy nor can I properly move about; if only they had seen me in my youth—now, there was a conflagration unbound!

Such sentimental reflection of tired souls expecting death washes the world over in diffident tidal waves every second, dying souls longing for glorious days past, tortured souls longing for impossibly glorious days future—yet the present populace does not seem to be honoring the passing of the generation before them, which laid the foundation for their good life; it is the unfurling story of birth to death, and nothing is supposed to interfere with the carefully programmed and rigid hands of the eternal clock—the old and feeble are supposed to be discarded like expired goods; it is what the world expects and demands so the youth of the world might go forward unimpeded by the moaning, cluttered and heavy spirits of a long-ago history.

The Silver Brook Retirement Home was not unlike every other place that had acquired the coveted role of intermediary between the dead and their inevitable destination afterward—like the boatman Charon who escorted souls across the River Styx, like the Pyramids built to house Pharaohs on their journey to the afterlife, like the Valkyrie flying the fallen Norse heroes to Valhalla—except that here it was a refuge to inhabit until the attendants found you disconnected from the living; here, the new resident arrived in one of several states: shuffling and retaining a mental acuity, hobbling and falling and having a brain-fogged stupor, or coming in as a walking cadaver; but in any condition the person came, they were fated to soon wither and die; and so another bed would become available, and then another body, bent and bowed, stiff and stale, and leaking the vital juices of life and stuffed with an exotic cocktail of powerful medicine, would arrive and slowly succumb to their last, inexorable breath. But perhaps some profiteer of exceeding acumen might chart the human births of the world every year and plot the number of people who survive into their final decrepit days and are unable to fend for themselves, and begin constructing enough retirement homes to contain them; but the truly ingenious moneymaker might look around the world and notice that technology was making life easier and therefore having a deleterious effect on the now longer-lasting human body through a complicated process known by its scientific name, *Profoundous lazinous*, thus creating even progressively younger captives, and build even more of these temporary hibernation chambers that would so engorge this cash cow that its golden milk fairly overflowed the coffers of these merchants of death.

Physicists have attempted for centuries to slow down time. All they needed do was come to the Silver Brook Recreation Retirement Home, for what was measured in seconds and minutes and hours on the outside was measured in days and weeks and months inside this mansion of moth-eaten, dust-and-cobweb-covered, rusted-through-and-through human beings. Anything or anyone entering this phantom paradise was slowed down, slowed down to a near standstill, slowed down to a grinding, groveling, excruciatingly painful crawl where gravity bulged and increased over them until they were as heavy as a heap of steel armor and still as granite mountains. The people here were soon caught up in the anti-life mesh which slowly pulled them toward a swirling vortex that led to the grave, for this place was unlike the outside world, which strives against ruin and embraces new things— in here there was an unclean spirit that settled upon every head and whispered into the ears of every person that life was over and they should never again hope for any new thing; the residents, then, were encased in a hot wax that was stuffed inside a cement cocoon, their joints having disintegrated and muscles having atrophied, their bones having become like peanut brittle, their spirits crumbled and crushed to dust as they envisioned their final trip to the metal urn.

This palace of lethargy and pain was unique in all the world, for here the people were not expected to improve their lot in life, not expected to improve their health, not expected to step back up to the challenges of the world and thrive; no, they were planted here out of pity, like an uprooted old tree with yellowing twigs that has served its purpose but must now make room for the young, green saplings; there was no hope here except the grim desire that the end would come swiftly and painlessly; *so, come, sweet messenger of death* was the unspoken refrain of the residents herein—*and come now*, was the pleading addendum.

If a resident fell, it was expected; if a resident moved, yes, they moved, as if with a heavy iron ball and chain attached to their spindly, sore-laden legs; a resident was fed and sheltered and protected the same way a condemned prisoner is who awaits execution; there was no joy here except in the remembrance of things past, but this was a joy no resident could sustain too long, for physical restraints always called them back to the awful present and cleansed their yearning mind of the glories of yesterday.

"I want to die," Mildred said in her raspy voice, smoothing out her pretty green-and-white-and-red-checkered cotton dress, "this body is worn out—I need a new one."

Martha smiled, but as fast as her wrinkled face lit up, it dimmed. "My children tell me to just keep living, but this isn't living, Mildred, it really isn't; now, when I was twenty and taking dancing lessons and singing on Broadway—my, my, now, that was living. Life is for the young, and I've had my moment."

"Poor Ruth," Mildred said, looking across the room to a woman in a wheelchair, "fell down last week and broke her hip—poor girl."

"And who is next?" Martha said, sadly. "I am afraid to stand up for fear of falling down; oh, it's all so embarrassing—and it all seems to wrong, doesn't it, that we have to end up like this. I sometimes wonder what my younger self would think if she saw me as I am now—would she even want me to have lived this long if I'm not doing anything except waiting around to die?"

"Every bone in my body aches."

"My teeth hurt."

Mildred and Martha laughed, and for one brief, wondrous, yet frightening moment, they were truly young again.

The women sat in close clusters on the first floor of the home, some of them with their minds gone and their bodies gone and their souls ready to flee; and the men sat in close clusters next to them, and some of them with their enthusiasm gone and their lust for life gone and their souls ready to flee.

"Where is Dolores?" Mary asked, confused.

"Why, she's dead, Mary," Sylvia said, holding the woman's bony, purple-blotched hands, and then looking at the entrance, she said, with an amusing smile, "Oh, look, here comes another lucky lottery winner."

In a slaughterhouse, one animal leaves in a thick plastic wrap while another animal arrives in a large steel truck; it is the way things are when your essential role in the grand scheme of things is greatly diminished and you are perceived as an increasing burden on society, with a corollary role that you exist for the monetary benefit of those who are circling above you in the black skies like bloodthirsty vultures who are drooling spit and avarice as you near the yielding up of your spirit.

"I liked Dolores," Mary said, frowning, "and she was a kind person, too."

Mary died a week later, and was effortlessly replaced—like a family replaces a dead dog—by Margery. No one stayed in this palace of eccentric relics too long, as this ghoulish haunt was not built to be a comfortable home but a living sepulcher. A lengthy existence for any resident here would have been a great inconvenience, for as the human body breaks down and cannot be repaired—or will not be repaired—it becomes increasingly difficult for caregivers to properly bring succor to such a body; it is like holding a wrecked car together with green duct tape and kite string and then driving down a winding road in the rain and sleet and snow.

So, one came in, ailing, spent, to stay for a while, while another finally and gratefully died—having exhausted all of their waning energies—died as they were scheduled to die; one in, one out, two in, two out, three in, three out; this was no workplace, no rehabilitation center, no boarding house, but a structure to contain the sick and dying, a structure existing to promote the furthering of body dissembling and the final closing of weary eyes; to come here meant body failure had pounced upon you and gripped you in its iron claws and swallowed your balding head into its black, oily mouth; bitter failure was what rode upon the faces of those trapped souls here, and success could be gained only through a welcomed death.

Gilbert had only recently tripped and stumbled over the seventh decade of life and yet was very ancient-looking, with his deeply wrinkled face, and very ancient feeling, with breath that was labored with every exertion as he moved with a slow gait inside his steel exoskeleton; but he had, he reckoned, lived a long life and was now ready for eternal peace.

One day, a new male resident came in and shuffled past him, and Gilbert looked at the man for a considerable time, even watching him as he was escorted to the elevator and up to his final resting place on earth—in his tiny cubicle, wherein he was expected to soon expire like a carton of milk with a long-overdue past-buy date; like the rest of his brethren here, he had not come for rejuvenation but termination.

"Manny," Gilbert whispered, knitting his bushy white eyebrows, "is it possible—Manny Gutierrez?" He turned round and slapped his thigh, and then winced in pain. "Good ol' Manny Gutierrez—why, I'll be! O boy—company on the last train out of town!"

Gilbert waited patiently for Manny to come down from the upstairs bunker that night, and the next day, too, until, finally, the crippled body of Manny came creeping down the stairs and soon settled onto a small velvet chair that rested on the drab white linoleum floor.

"O, boy, Manny, here I come, O boy," Gilbert whispered joyously, and upon standing—that is, upon attempting to stand, which took some time, as he had very little arm and thigh muscle to properly propel himself upward—he shuffled his red-slipper-covered feet and crooked body over to his boyhood pal. He carefully sat down next to him, and once he had resumed his regularly scheduled breathing, said, excitedly, "Manny Gutierrez!"

Manny had already nodded off to sleep. "Huh, what, time for bed already?" he stammered. "Time for pills again?"

"Manny, do you remember me, old buddy, huh, Manny?"

Manny focused his dry, bloodshot eyes at the accosting gentlemen, and then casually shook his head as if he were responding to a door-to-door salesman. "Nope."

"Oh, Manny, for shame! It's me!" he exclaimed, flabby arms open wide. "Your old pal!"

Manny focused once again, shook his full head of grey hair, then put on his eyeglasses and looked very, very hard at this man, and then said very honestly, "Nope."

"Manny Gutierrez, you lame-brained, knuckleheaded, skinny mamma's boy!"

"Gilbert!" he cried.

The two old friends embraced, incurring a bruise on each of their swollen backs.

"There isn't anyone I would rather share my living coffin with than you, Gil, old buddy," Manny said, smiling largely now.

"Always the wise guy," Gilbert returned, wiping away tears that struggled down the rolls of his sagging brown flesh.

The two men talked of things long since passed, of people and things, and events and epochs; of their separation after high school and married life and deaths and social upheavals; and yet, they were fated to reminisce about the time when first they met.

"Mr. Wyatt!" they both exclaimed.

"What a rebellious spirit," Gilbert said, his hazel-colored eyes ablaze with awe and respect.

"An iconoclast to the end," Manny said.

"A sixth-grade Teacher who taught us more about life than even our parents," Gilbert stated, his voice suffused with admiration.

"A man who lived his ideals—a man who joined the war effort even though he did not have to…" There was nothing more to say here lest both men break down and sob like little children.

"And to those who listened, we were set off on our greatest adventure," Gilbert reflected.

"And to think he was always there for us, even after we went to junior high," Manny said.

Gilbert smiled. "Remember how he used to say that we would not remember the tests he gave us or the curriculum we learned, but only those important things pertaining to life?"

"And here we are—over sixty years later, and we remember what he said. Remarkable!"

"Amazing," Gilbert said, but he soon became perplexed, and then his voice grew heavy, and his tone, and his expression, fearful, "and yet here we are, but we shouldn't be." The men sat quietly for a moment, pondering this eerie pronouncement. "There was something he said once, do you remember it—there was something he said once about all of us remembering about the far distant future..."

There always seems to be a small, important something that is buried in the deep recesses of a long-ago past that people will occasionally attempt to locate; sometimes it is an event or thing or person that brings about the planting of a very special seed in their memories; sometimes it is meant to nestle there, like a good shepherd who watches the flock and awaits the call to market; and sometimes it is buried there, like a sleeping amphibian who lies in its silent chambers just below the surface of the soil and who patiently waits for the drought to be usurped by precious rain to finally awaken it; and very old people have many, many good and faithful shepherds awaiting the signal, and many, many dormant amphibians awaiting that first soft kiss of rain, but may have neglected to build a proper house for such delicate memories to reside in, so when the light vapors of such a memory arise in their mind and they taste and smell its unique essence and search for it, they find the skeletal remains burnt in a consuming fire that leaves only a faded shadow scorched into the multilayered scars of days gone by.

Gilbert and Manny had seized upon the small seed and watered it and nourished it; for days they did this, truly they did—for days they talked of the entire history of Mr. Wyatt and their fellow students, and in this way they were like those brave men who throw great steel grappling hooks from small boats into freezing waters to look for things once alive; and so, in this fashion the two old friends were able to grab hold of fragments of the past and bring them to the surface and with great effort haul them on board with their dry, aching hands, catching fleeting bits of debris and ensnaring chunks and splinters and even floating bits of dust, then assembling that which had been so long ago dissembled.

"He used to say we would not remember the curriculum," Gilbert stated, confidently.

"That much is established," Manny said, assuredly.

Gilbert held up his index finger. "He said we would remember only the important things pertaining to life."

"Yes," Manny said, "and only those things that were important to our well-being, like how to think about the world…"

"Yes, and how to properly live in a world that teaches you about all the wrong things—that we must constantly question everything, and ask questions of everything."

"Yes, and how to properly live…"

"And that we are here for each other, and to love one another," Gilbert said, and then paused for a moment, and then added, "as he loved us, unconditionally…"

"This is wisdom that has stayed with me always—but there is something else he said one day, only one day, I know it was something about the far distant future..."

Gilbert screwed up his face as he ran his wrinkled hands over his thick, grey hair, and then whispered, "But what, what," and he closed his misty eyes, "what was it...?"

"What," Manny murmured, closing his azure-colored eyes, "what treasures did he bury in our consciousness so long ago to awaken us even now, one more gift he bestowed upon us..."

"He planned our future..."

"How...?"

And so in this prolonged and advanced trance state, the two men meditated upon the inexhaustible, the immutable, the inviolate concepts that had served them so well all their lives and cross-referenced them to what Mr. Wyatt had said, but found no good luck therein; and so, in this inward-leaning brain scouring, they failed.

"Gone," Gilbert declared, throwing up his arms.

Manny was still staring into the charitable images of the past when his wizened face lit up like the northern star on a clear Summer night. "We shall find another!"

"Another of us!"

And so the men examined the available public records and soon found one of their old classmates living nearby, and after contacting her, she was there in a slowed-down and barely audible heartbeat.

"Margaret Rasmussen!" the boys declared when—at least to their own eyes—their still young and beautiful Margaret came quickstepping up to them with her brown wooden cane as trusty sidekick; and after the requisite hugs and kisses and tears and excited talk of old days and friends was explored, the boys, for this is what they truly were in the presence of a woman they had both loved in their youth, inquired if she knew about the cryptic message Mr. Wyatt had planted skillfully in their forming minds so long ago.

Margaret had always been the sharpest one in the class, and somehow, over the long years and despite the assaults from chemical and personal warfare upon her person, her mind had been protected and was remarkably free from serious defects and was still fully functional. It did not take her long to summon the stealthy message to the surface of her memories.

She was wearing a considerable amount of makeup but it had been expertly applied so that it did not look like it had been painted with a heavy brush on an old leathery bag that had been left out in the scorching sun too long. "You know, I hadn't really thought of it, but now that you handsome boys are sitting next to me—I do, I do remember what he said." She frowned as she looked about. "Oh, but this place is so dreary and stuffy," and here she wiggled her bare, brown, slender shoulders; "seeing this human petrified forest gives me the creeps," and she leaned over to them and whispered, "all of these old people just sitting around and talking about nothing because in the back of their minds they don't want to talk about that something called death," and she leaned back and smiled. "My throat is dry— how about a glass of sherry and a little music, eh, fellas?"

"Margaret," Manny smiled affectionately, "you daughter of a gun."

She laughed and then became serious as she thrust out her ring-laden hand. "Mr. Wyatt would call me that all the time and poor Cindy Thompson would let the little ol' green-eyed monster of jealousy just drive her wild—and it didn't matter to her even when he would say that anyone who is a good student is really the Teacher's pet; she just couldn't take the fact that there was someone in the room he doted on other than her pretty little self." She smiled largely and warmly at the sweet remembrance of it all. "Mr. Wyatt was the best Teacher we ever had—no, he was the best Teacher any of us could have ever had—and isn't it so funny that we sort of knew it at the time, too, like we could, even as children, recognize when someone is teaching us things about the world we need to know and in a way that sings to our adolescent soul." She nodded her head and her rich brown ponytail flowed over her naked back as she closed her emerald-colored eyes, and her body swayed to and fro as she hummed a tune he had taught them in a magical world that had been created by one man willing to teach and by thirty students willing to learn. But then the reverie was soon broken and she opened up her eyes and said, snapping her fingers, "Now, what about that sherry, boys—don't you just have to wash away the bad taste this place gives you once in a while?"

"Gosh, is that a rhetorical question?" Manny said, amusingly.

"No!" Margaret said, nearly irritated, looking around at the languid eyes and impoverished faces of the residents as they talked in their small groups on this bottom floor. "It's so depressing in here!"

"But we live here, Margaret, it isn't like we have a choice."

"Oh, fiddlesticks, Gil, everyone has a choice in their own home—and I don't care who your little Miss Tyrannical-Overseer is," she began, and then smiled mischievously as she leaned over to them and whispered, "I'll be right back—and meet me in Manny's suite in twenty."

The boys watched the old gal scoot away. "Crazy then, crazy now," Gilbert said.

"And still hot," Manny whispered, raising his sparse eyebrows twice in weak succession.

In twenty minutes' time a silly announcement came, as evidenced by a ridiculous knock-knock and then, in rapid succession, knock-knock-knock, and this was followed by a brief pause, and once more a knock-knock banged on the door of Manny's pad.

"Refreshments!" Margaret announced, pulling out a large bottle of sherry from a big black leather purse. "Let's rock and roll, boys!"

"You were never one for the rules," Gilbert said, uneasily.

"Oh, rules—phooey," she returned, waving said rules away by a hand with five brightly colored metallic bracelets on the wrist, "rules are made by old fuddy-duddies—boring people who are afraid to do anything they might fail at or get hurt doing." She turned on the small radio that sat atop Gilbert's small maple desk and plopped in a cassette, and then turned it on, and out came loud and abusive rock and roll music, which Gilbert immediately turned down. "Geez, it's like living in a mausoleum around here, fellas—I mean, you're all going to die soon anyway, so why not go out doing whatever makes you happy!"

"Such compassion," Gilbert replied, somewhat vexed.

Margaret waved him off easily with the flick of her hand, and then, smiling knowingly, reached into her seemingly bottomless purse and pulled out a small black leather book that was inside a plastic baggie. "Diary," she whispered, raising her penciled brown eyebrows, and then taking a sip of the delicious straw-colored wine, "drink up, fellas, you're going to need it."

"A diary, eh," Manny said, his eyes squinting at the object, "how perfectly female!"

"How perfectly smart," she exclaimed. "This is a doggone walking history book," and she leaned over and whispered,

"I've got the goods on some of the most famous men in America—slept with them all, too," and she winked, playfully.

Gilbert had a sour face when he said in a stern manner, "Do you really think anyone would really care about the sexual exploits of people that long ago—and with a commoner, too?"

She smiled at Gilbert as if she expected his acrimonious spirit to attempt to ensnare her, but she was properly armed and ready for it. "Oh, Gilbert," she said, smiling, "you're just a barrel of laughs—always thinking," and she pointed right at him, "class president and captain of the football team in high school, and always the thinker about important issues," and she pointed to her head, "that's why you need ol' Margaret here to bail you out, you old thinker, you!"

"All right, I give—but just skip the parts about J. Edgar Hoover and Stalin…"

Her smile dissipated and was replaced by disappointment. "You're just plain ol' mean sometimes, Gilbert—I mean, a girl can ignore only so much. So what in the world happened to you? You used to be mean—and happy."

His hard countenance dropped in the absence of her malice, and when he spoke, it was a voice immersed in defeat and struggle, as he gesticulated about. "Oh, I don't know, it's just living in this jolly place that cheers a guy up."

She reached out her hand and placed it tenderly on his. "How did you ever wind up in here, anyway, huh?"

Gilbert, reluctantly, after much cajoling by her, related the last sad years of his once-spectacular life—a wife dead, a business dead, his two children estranged from him—and his inevitable fall from independent man of means to a dependent cripple soaked in poverty and despair.

"And you, Manny?" she asked, in earnest.

Manny had lost his wife long ago, and ever since he had lost his ability to move about without worry of bodily injury, his children had lobbied to send him here, and so here he was.

"Humph!" she exclaimed, looking about, and then pointing to herself, "I'll die before they cage this tigress."

"I believe you," Manny said, nodding his round head and staring with affection at her defiant and beautiful gestures.

"Now, for a girl's best friend," she said, smiling again as she unzipped the plastic bag and carefully extracted the black leather-bound book, "let's see what we can see."

"Really, I don't see what a diary…" Gilbert began, but she reached out and placed two long, slender fingers on his lips.

She said, passionately, "Hush, darling, and you will hear the midnight reading of Margaret's tears," and took another sip of the fermented grape juice, and then melancholically, "even good girls write down what they know is most important to them at the time, like when Mr. Wyatt told us a great secret that I transcribed as soon as I went out to recess, and then went home and copied onto my precious scrolls," and she patted the faded cover and hugged the book to her bosom as if it were a living creature needing affection. Manny and Gilbert looked on in utter fascination.

"Let us see, then, what we can see, and reveal the truths hidden therein," she whispered, opening the book and slowly turning the pages with great ceremony, her eyes luminous like stones of beryl green. "Good stuff; good, ripe gossip, this," she murmured to herself, scrunching up her cute little upturned nose.

"Well, I mean, would it hurt to know at least some of it?" Manny asked, innocently.

Gilbert was incredulous. "Manny, you're still worried about whether or not Joe met Sally at the park and kissed her. I mean, come on, ol' buddy—it's over!"

Margaret ushered a sly smile and whispered, "I know who kissed Debbie Dyer behind the stadium in seventh grade."

The face of Gilbert lit up like a lamp. "Who? Who did what? I loved that girl! Who was the lecherous rat?"

Margaret smiled and raised her brown eyes brows. "Joshua Johnson."

"Joshua Johnson! That wussy! She kissed him when she said she loved only me!"

Margaret smiled knowingly at Manny, who smiled in return.

More revelations poured out of the little black book of horrors, and more outrages came back from the boys, and then more revelations came and more hilarity came back, until the curiosity of all was satiated, and the real prize came forthwith.

"And then on May fifth, Mr. Wyatt, after having Wendy Springer turn off the lights…"

"I always wondered what happened to her," Manny said, politely.

"Dead—overdose. Come on now, hippie generation," she replied plainly. Manny sat, dejected. She read now, slowly, carefully, as if she were looking for word traps wherein lay hidden memory bombs, "…After having Wendy Springer turn off the lights, he made us shut our eyes—I wonder why he is doing that now—but then he said in a low voice as he walked around the room:

"'One day, a very long time from now that is inconceivable to you, when you are very, very old, and you are sitting in a wheelchair or are living in a retirement home and you are absolutely certain there is no way back to this great time in your magical lives, I want you to think of this moment, this very, precise moment—I am planting this lucid memory in your minds so you can have a way back from oblivion; listen to me, children, where you are then, you do not have to be, you only think you have to be because of the terrible lie society has given you—but you don't have to suffer anymore. Listen to me very carefully, children: you don't have to be weak and useless and have soft bones and lose your muscle and have all kinds of diseases—this is the picture painted by people of this modern age who do not exercise and eat right, and who do not know how to think—remember, it doesn't matter what everyone else is doing, even if all of them are doing the wrong thing and it seems that you are the only one doing what you know is the right thing; you do what you need to do to take care of yourself. Listen, children, listen and remember,' he shouted at us—why? 'If you run and jump, and hop and skip and dart and dive, if you lift and pull and push and throw, and eat natural food, peasant food, real, unprocessed food that was meant to be planted, harvested, prepared and then eaten, you can go home again.' He walked around the room silently for a minute, and when he spoke again, his voice was urgent and desperate, as if there was a great calamity upon us, 'That which is bent, can be unbent; the road that is crooked, can be made straight again; that which is broken, can be fixed; the body wants to heal—always—it is never too late; never! Do not listen to those who would tell you to give up—so remember, and live life to the fullest even when you are ninety or a hundred and two!'"

She stopped reading.

"Pretty cryptic, huh?" Margaret whispered, her eyes screwed up in fascination.

"What does it all mean, anyway?" Manny asked, excitedly.

When Margaret had begun to read, Gilbert was transported back to the very place and exact moment of Mr. Wyatt's foretelling of the future, and he could see the forever-young, black-haired, muscular Mr. Wyatt walking around the room, he truly could—he could see his classmates and he could feel his own strong muscles and vibrant youth returning and he could feel the boundless energy they had all felt every day that school year; and as she quit reading so abruptly, abruptly the connection his mind had made was severed and yanked rudely back and he felt his youth drain away from him and he could feel his bones and muscles stiffen and his senses dull. There was a look of revelation upon his animated visage. "It means," he murmured, so low that his two friends had to lean closer to him to listen, "that he provided a way back for us even when he knew he could not be there for us," and his eyes misted and his countenance was joyous, "he was truly our friend, for he cared for us all of our lives." The three friends sat and contemplated this for a moment, and then Gilbert sang, "But it all means we're getting out of this place, if it's the last thing I ever do."

"O, The Animals," Margaret said, giggling, "sexy!"

"Do you really think we can do it, huh?" Manny asked, and then turning toward Margaret, "You know, that was rather remarkable for a twelve-year-old to write down."

For a brief lull, the faces of the boys sank at the idea she had fabricated the whole affair, and then the ever-present shrill voices of the naysayers rose in their minds, telling them all was indeed lost and that she had lain down a road to follow they knew was a lie.

"So, you don't trust me, eh?" she returned, leaning back in her chair, and then sipping some more sherry. "But I suppose it is normal, after all, I was just a kid at the time—but not just an ordinary kid; oh, no, no way—because after he said all of that," and then she leaned over and smiled at them as does the one who knows they have won before the game has begun, "I just clicked off the tape recorder."

"You taped Mr. Wyatt!" Manny shouted.

"Well, really, I was taping Wendy Springer, who is dead now, by the way—and no, God," she cried, and looked upward and clasped her hands, "please do not rest her soul until she repents," and then she looked back to the boys again, "for weeks, and I just happened to have it with me that day; now, I did write down everything he said word for word, but later I kind of dressed up my narrative a little bit," and she put out the index finger and thumb of her right hand to make a little space.

"It's unbelievable that you secretly taped us," Gilbert said.

"Of all the nerve," Manny exclaimed.

"Would you rather I had thrown it away, huh?"

"Well, no, but still," Manny answered, and then rubbing his whiskered chin, "did you happen to tape anyone else?"

"Oh, for goodness' sake, Manny," Gilbert said, exasperated, "you're still twelve years old!"

Manny ignored him and urged her to continue on, and she then said, "No, not really, most of it was just meaningless chatter, really—and by the way, just in case you're wondering, the tapes broke long ago and I threw them all away."

"All!" he said, sadly.

"Oh, sure—about twenty, I think."

Manny was flabbergasted. "Did you work for Nixon, huh?"

She smiled, knowingly. "O, the stories I could tell you about that tricky administration…"

Her smile liberated any shock from the face of Manny.

Gilbert, wide-eyed and bushy-tailed now, and alive with the sound of music that logic makes when it is soaring on the hot columns of wisdom, stated emphatically, "I have a plan," and then carefully and succinctly he laid it out before them, and when it was done, his two old classmates were thunderstruck. "We're going to push and pull and run and jump our way right of this 'way station' to the grave," he finished, smiling strongly, his eyes looking back and forth to his friends, "and the answer has been right there in front of us the entire time—and this is no dream, no fancy; this is science, as Mr. Wyatt taught us—and I have known it all along but did not remember his lessons on how to think about such issues." He stood up and cried, "Who is with me?"

"We are," Margaret and Manny shouted, too standing up, and then all three of them placed a hand atop the hand of the other, a symbolic act they had often practiced during that magical year in sixth grade.

Gilbert picked up the opaque black bottle with his weak and slightly arthritic hands and poured the sweet wine into the three crystal goblets, and then raising his glass to the glasses of his friends, he said, solemnly, "To Mr. Wyatt, who is with us now and forever."

"To Mr. Wyatt, who will always be older and wiser than I," Manny said.

"To Mr. Wyatt, who gave us love and heart and soul," Margaret said.

And the three friends clanked glasses together and sipped the chilled wine, and then talked long, long into the grand, good night about old times and old friends, and they dismissed the lights-out alarm and were very quiet when the attendants came looking for the missing woman who was presumably still on the premises; and for a moment, they were children again who knew that being mischievous made them feel more alive than when they followed the same old boring rules.

Finally, Margaret crept out of the boy's room at six in the a.m., and later that night, in her small apartment, she was gently sobbing and slowly drinking, and she whispered, her head on her folded arms on her tiny, wooden desk, "A girl has to have some secrets," and she slid her right thumb into her warm, moist mouth, and mumbled, "I should never have outlived my usefulness and my limited fortune—one must know the proper place and time to die and follow the proper rules to attain immortality on earth," and she gently pressed the button on the player and heard the low passionate whisper which rose to a thundering and plowing voice that rumbled and tumbled throughout her small dark apartment.

"One day, a very long time from now that is inconceivable to you, when you are very, very old and you are sitting in a wheelchair or are living in a retirement home and you are absolutely certain there is no way back to this great moment in your magical lives…"

\* \* \* \* \*

"It's here, the package is here," Gilbert whispered to Manny as he wheeled himself up to his friend on the downstairs "floor of complacency," as they now deemed it; the men quickly agreed to open the package in the privacy of their rooms, but not in Gilbert's room, as he was somewhat of a hoarder and averse to structure and order.

"One bit at a time, we smuggle it in—how pathetic is that!" Manny said, excitedly, as he and Gilbert lingered too long to undo the tidy and tightly bound big brown package; but finally the brown parcel was peeled open to reveal the prizes therein. "*Building Strength and Muscle*," he whispered, as if in a shrine, as if the book itself had been sent down from the heavens.

"Ice-blue handgrips," Gilbert whispered, his eyes wide open, just as if he were a kid again and he was opening presents on his eighth birthday party, "the beginning of the end for flaccid and decaying muscles." He picked up the grips but, alas, he could not close one even with two hands. "Say, Manny, give me a hand here; I think this one must be stuck or something..." Manny placed his hands over Gilbert's hands and both men strained with all of their available might to close the mocking apparatus, but both men failed, not getting it to budge even one disturbing inch.

"Dang thing must be broken," Manny exclaimed, breathless.

"Dang thing," Gilbert echoed, breathless too, and then they looked each other full in the perspiring face of the other as he said, "or we are."

"Huh? We're that weak—no way!"

Gilbert reached over and took the copious papers on exercise and nutrition he had collected off the Internet and set them on the small brown table before them and then put the handgrip exercisers on this manila folder. "Manny, we're still living as if we are young bucks and able to do what men with muscle can do, but I have a news flash for you—we aren't!" And he looked to the handgrips. "It's us, Manny; we are that weak," and then his voice dropped off as if he had just looked into a mirror that was not dark and foggy and realized he was very old and not apt to get any younger, "it's us..."

"You mean we think we're fifty-year-old youngsters, right?" he said, hopefully.

"No, I mean like a ten-year-old; when we were ten, don't you remember—we had things like this, and we could close that grip," and he attempted to snap his fingers but failed miserably, "like it was nothing."

Manny contemplated this epiphany and then blew out a stormy, "Shoot!"

"Exactly."

"But is it too late?"

"Heck, if it is—but if it were over, that would mean there are no miracles in life and everything is inevitable; but ah, Manny, if just one person can walk backward into the fabled fountain and recover one cell thought lost…"

"I can see Mr. Wyatt telling us never to believe what we see and hear because what we see and hear comes down from people who do not know how to see and do not know how to hear, and that whatever they have heard from great minds they often confuse—now, when you are falling over the cliff, you definitely want someone to pull you back…"

The men closed their eyes and allowed the gentle sagacity of their Teacher to stroke their tired bodies.

"Gilbert," Manny whispered, opening his eyes again, "do you think we'll ever be young again?"

Gilbert, staring now at the stiff-as-frozen-stout-tree-limbs handgrips, evinced a countenance as if it had intercepted and fully utilized the eternal waves of hope and determination that had created the greatest civilizations of history past; and so, he picked up the hard plastic prongs with both of his bony, flabby hands and then he squeezed with all of his feeble might, and when it became apparent to Manny that the impossible was near the possible—that the stubborn grip was yielding to the strength of the man, albeit only slightly—and that this was the most the man might do now, Manny enjoined his hands atop the hands of his friend and he too pushed with all of his feeble strength; and lo, that stiff, hard blue grip really began to bend, just like a tree sapling might be pulled down by a pair of strong men—at least this is the analogy the two friends would have felt appropriate now.

And when the small victory was over—the obstinate grip had closed at least halfway—and the boys had proclaimed victory with a whoop and a slap of their bruised hands against each other, Gilbert said, enthusiastically, "Maybe we will not be young again, Manny old friend, but we will be younger, much, much younger..."

The very first step back from living with eyes sealed shut in a closing grave is as important as a baby's first step toward a promised land wherein dwells freedom and discovery; and every step taken, be it fair or fumbling, lean or fat, high or low, increases the mind and body unity and one's devotion to pursuing more steps, unlimited steps, bold and fast steps toward adventure; so, just as no respectable tree puts out healthy branches toward the nourishing yellow sun and feels the great energy of life surging through its roots and bursting into its slender brown corrugated trunk and sturdy limbs and into its very sweet and tender leaves, and then decides to throw down its high arms to the dark valley of cold shadows to feast on the moldy carcass of spoilage and in so doing kills itself, so too those courageously back from death, and the sojourning baby, too, will not yield to illogic or even stubborn barriers—for those things that overcome our travelers, by those things are they enslaved.

A plain paper package would come for Manny one week and another for Gilbert the next, and then Margaret would come in bearing gifts—as much as her weak hands could carry—and the program of stealth and strength was ripening, just like a sweet Georgia peach in springtime.

Disaster struck like a naval ship in heavily mined waters during an exercise session that was led by the fitness and nutrition program coordinator at the retirement home. Gilbert called the session "Self-delusion and how to die faster."

"All right, ladies and gentlemen," the heavyset woman in the grey sweats said, and like a match half-lit her voice was in power and intent, as if she meant only to move the people before her only part of the way toward anything meaningful because that was all she perceived their worth to be—an inch, and not a mile; and the twelve residents who were either in a wheelchair or supported by a cane or were sitting their fossilized bodies before her were eerily quiet as she moved her hulking form about the place, "are we ready to exercise today?"

"Does that mean you and us, or just us?" a woman asked, innocently.

The instructor issued an exasperated look and shook her head. "Come on, ladies," she shouted, as she huffed and puffed her corpulent form around the sauna-like room, "come on, gentlemen," she bellowed, raising her chubby hands on high, as it seemed only she could; but it would have been easier to raise the dead with a My First Electrical Conductor Set then levitate the hands of these prisoners who had muscle in arms as thin as reeds and flab hanging off their bodies like dripping silly putty.

And then during this unremarkable display of death's jaw clamping down further upon the crumbling skeleton and shriveling muscles of the dead souls therein, a most remarkable event occurred.

A three-pound black polyester and Velcro wristband crashed to the semi-imitation cherry-colored wood with a curious crack, snap and pop.

Miss All-Retirement-Home-Exercise-Guru abated her pseudo-arduous exercise regimen just as if someone's teeth had inadvertently plopped to the wooden floor; and frowning mightily, with her eyes screwed up, she approached the inopportune intruder as if it now had taken on the form of a black mamba. "Outrageous!" she exclaimed, stopping over the weird object in question, her feet on her fat hips and thighs. The rest of the dying carousel looked on in wild wonder. "How in the world did that," she cried, her mouth agape, "get in here?" She looked up as if to examine the blond stucco ceiling for holes—as did the complaint prisoners—and then she looked down again at the still object—as did her curious prisoners—and then, like a cautious snake catcher, she slowly bent down and extended two fingers of her right hand and retrieved the Velcro band and held it up as if now it had transformed itself into a dead, stinking mouse; but now, her fat, dirty-brown eyes narrowed as she looked round for the smug and reticent infidel who had thrashed and pummeled her sense of fair play and impaired her judgment—at least, as she knew them to be. "All right," she began, like a punishing prosecutor, her hand, like the flaming sword of vengeance, raised now against her bewildered audience, "whose is this; come on now, good friends, 'fess up."

O, to have beheld the sea of grey and fuzzy white heads, with their respective quizzical faces, and the frail, hump-backed, bent-over, bone-as-strong-as-powder-paste-in-hollowed-out-twig-like bodies, one would have decided she was more machine than human. She might as well have been interrogating the cat about the whereabouts of the dog's tasty white soup bones.

"What now, sweetie," gentle Ruth Huxley said, every one of her ninety-one years of age apparent in her wobbling soft voice, "who are you looking for?"

"The culprit, Ruth," Miss Exercise growled, now holding up the evidence with her index finger and thumb and dangling it in the air as if it were contagious, "the culprit responsible," and then, shaking said evidence, "for this."

"Eh, what's that, Miss Vickers?" Winston O'Connell asked, in his barely audible voice as he cupped his shaking hand to his long ear. "Who are you looking for?"

Vexed now that an infraction had occurred and had not been immediately resolved, Miss Vickers, as if by an unseen collusion, began to stomp around the soft carpet while still dangling the weight in her hand. "A clear violation of the rules, this," she cried in a guttural tone, "and oh yes, we have rules here, people, we do, and for a reason—someone might get hurt wearing this little booby trap on their ankle; bones might break—crack!" she shouted, imitating with her chubby, sweaty hands in a vicious clap said bone being snapped in two. "So, if there is one of these little infractions floating about, my little pretty," she said, her voice pared down to a weird, prying chant, "then there must be a second one among you—a twin! Aha! So, there we have it—all of you," she thrust out her hands toward them, "lift up your pant legs!"

"Are we going to cancan?" sweetheart Mabel Perkins asked, innocently, smiling. "It's been so long, but I believe I am able," she finished, her fingers running along her bottom lip now.

"Oh, quiet, Mabel, and lift up your pant legs, you naughty girl!"

"But I'm so shy," she replied, blushing and turning from side to side, her hands folded together in front of her, "only my handsome groom has even seen my slender ankles."

"Oh, for goodness' sake, Mabel, what century are you living in—and you're stalling, to boot!"

"But I cannot seem to lift my pant legs," protested Harold Bingham weakly as he attempted to bend over but failed.

"Oh, for goodness' sake, Harold," Miss Vickers declared, and as she bent over to lift up his sweat pants, another thudding of something dropped onto the floor occurred.

"Eh, what's that?" Miss Vickers shouted, and turning around, saw another black Velcro-covered ankle weight sitting on the wooden floor behind her. "Egad! Another one! Who threw that? Who? Tell me or I'll cut your rations!"

Gilbert leaned over and whispered to Manny, "She thinks we're prisoners of war."

"We are," Manny whispered back, "and our tunneling has just begun."

Later that night, after the lights-out signal, Manny crept stealthily into Gilbert's room, and the two men engaged in a session of unbridled mirth for several minutes, laughing so loudly that they were coerced to smash their faces into the green fluffy pillows to muffle the silly clamor.

"Oh, that Miss Vickers." Manny smiled, wiping the tears of joy from his eyes. "She's a caution."

"Doggone strap, though," Gilbert said, giggling still, "broke free while I was exercising—so, from now on, no ankle weights around the commandant!"

It was a strict rule in the Silver Brook Retirement Home that no resident might pick up or even acquire an object that by its very shape or weight or surface might bring grievous harm or injury to that resident.

"It's absolutely ridiculous that we have to smuggle in weights," Manny declared, after performing his twelve proper push-ups—it that had taken him three months to complete just one such push-up—and after wiping his white eyebrows, "it's like a P.O.W. camp around here—hey, we might as well start constructing an escape tunnel." He smiled now, and when Gilbert, who was practicing his handstand push-ups, which had taken him thirteen months to perfect, smiled, he knew he had to pad his silly scenario, and so he feigned a somber voice. "All right, we'll wear stockings inside our pant legs and fill them with dirt and then will empty it outside in the garden and then rake it into the ground; of course, we'll have to have our confederates singing loudly while we are digging."

Gilbert collapsed and laughed while he propped himself up on his slender-albeit-now-muscular arms. "Stupid rules—but hey, we have Margaret, who has never known a rule she couldn't subvert."

"But we still have to hide the weights from the faculty—say, you've seen those prison movies," he began, nearly giggling as he ran to the sink and looked under it, "don't they always hide contraband in the walls, inside false compartments?"

"We could just continue to hide the weights between the mattresses."

"But where is the fun in that? Where is the struggle, the challenge?"

"But I don't want a struggle or a challenge, I just want out; but we do need a plan…"

"That is exactly what I am saying, Gil, we need to do something—we have too many weights to hide now, and I'm not sleeping on lumps!"

Margaret arrived later, and with her, five more pounds of black steel weights and two light aluminum dumbbells, and a devious stratagem.

A week hence, when the staff came in to clean and inspect the rooms, they saw weird-looking model cars made out of painted aluminum tubes for shafts and steel plates for wheels and stacked plastic weights as the body, and as the main body was draped with classic Model T frames, they could not take in the whole package and unpack it and separate what was common and what was not, and what was necessary and what was not, and certainly they never considered the idea of the men using the weights for lifting—no, this heretical act never entered into their minds, and so when they left, no one was the wiser.

And so, the road to redemption was now unobstructed, and a daily schedule of workouts and proper nutrition—based on copious books the men had bought and borrowed, and articles they had read in muscle and strength magazines and on reputable strength-training websites, and on strength and fitness coaches they had consulted on the phone and even a few they had visited—was strictly adhered to; the proper clothes were worn by the men at the proper time around other residents and staff so as to mask the carving away of the old, diseased, sagging flesh that was being replaced with their new, vibrant, toned muscle, and the two men moved in the same non-threatening, dilapidated manner so as to damper any suspicion about their rejuvenating bodies; however, a rising star cannot yield itself to the ground for too long, and oftentimes at night, two now intrepid youths would flirt with danger and race about the place, in costume, in disguise, flying up and down the stairs, jumping up and over chairs, sliding down the polished handrails, sliding down the waxen floors, crawling and somersaulting and hand-walking over the thin blue carpet, until a disturbed staff member might hear the commotion and come to check on the clamor and quake, only to find flitting shadows disappearing into the misty veil of darkness.

Even as the two newly regenerating athletes increased their muscle mass and decreased their layers of dangerous fat, even as they soared ever upward toward rarified air occupied by only a few of their generation, even as they ate a diet of fresh fruits and vegetables, raw nuts and seeds, a variety of legumes, whole grains, wild-caught salmon, and egg whites, and revitalized their bodies, they made errors—yes, they

injured themselves on the way up and had to take a step downward, but this was acceptable and expected; even as they found
the finest foods and experienced the finest health, they made
errors in their selection, which was acceptable and expected;
but in the end, they settled on the exercises that would help
them and not hurt them, and the foods that would boost their
energy and impart radiant health to them. And as this happened, as they regressed in their very morbid state to a state of
vitality and robustness, they were no longer able to spend the
majority of their time in this deteriorating time machine, and
began to spend many hours a day in the park where they power
walked and ran, skipped rope, practiced moving through their
parkour obstacle courses, and performed their body weight
exercises; or at the local gym where they pushed weights and
swam and rowed, or the local library or health food store, or
anywhere they could be unleashed and do what they had once
done—live; and on their travels, which soon began from the
first bright flash of rosy sunup and ended at the smoky eclipse
of sundown, they encountered citizens of their own age. Once,
when they would have been in perfect synchronization with
this species of human that in the end—because of a paucity
of exercise, because of a poor diet, and because of these things
they seemed to dissolve like a burning wick every day—began
to look all the same, despite what they looked like ten, twenty
or even thirty long-forgotten years ago, as if all of their divers
shapes and comeliness and physical features were scraped away
until they were now all virtual replicas; for they were all of the
same stiff, mottled clay—white-or-grey-haired, stooped-over,
slow-walking, of a confused countenance, trembling, fearful,
feeble, an army of the walking dead that seemed to come from
one uncommon mold. Was this us, the two newly minted
creatures would say in wild wonder, is it possible that we could

not hold up a mirror and see what we had become, and what we could truly be? What lie was told to us that our minds were deceived, and our hearts so accepting of defeat—we, the generation that built up this country with our indomitable spirit and unquenchable desire to create a harmonious society? How could we be so fooled, and so abandoned, and yet, so culpable; we, who deserve so much better?

And yet the men stayed in this human glue factory, for they had a mission beyond that of their own mind and body.

It was sometime later when Miranda Salcido, she of the great Salcido clan of San Jose, who had once ruled that enclave but had lately fallen like a statue into dust and rubble, noticed something awry in her tight world where all images and icons were juxtaposed, where the smallest detail out of the smallest alignment would be sorely exposed, so crammed into this steel and concrete cell were she and her new, albeit, poorer clan. "You know," she said, frowning, and leaning over to her new best friend, Millicent—her other best friends in the last six months, Betty, Wilma, Martha and Maria, had all died—while the two women played bridge at the downstairs table in the morning, "I seem to remember that irascible Gilbert walking as slow as Grandma's molasses, and now I could have sworn that I saw him nearly running up the stairs the other day; isn't that simply wild? And he looks younger, too!"

"Oh, folderol," Edna the eavesdropper interjected, feigning to concentrate on her cards, "play the game, Miranda—you're hallucinating."

"No, she isn't," Millicent said, "I have seen him fairly stomping about—with his cute little brother, Manny! And yes, he looks younger, too!"

"Oh, nonsense and peppermint," Edna said, waving away the entire specter of speculation with her bejeweled, green-veins-popping-through-like-snakes hand, "you're all having flashbacks from the sixties—and I hope you're laying off the weed these days; for shame!"

"Well," Millicent declared, "I'll have you know I haven't smoked Mary Jane in twenty-four hours; so, I suppose my head is as clear as fine crystal."

Edna squinted through her bifocals at the woman. "Twenty-four hours, you say? Is that all, sweetie—geez!"

"Oh, Edna, you old fuddy-duddy, you could always get high with a little help from your friends—it couldn't hurt!" Millicent said, amused, remembering her unrestrained days of frivolous youth and living on candy-colored rainbows and soothing soul music.

"A proper lady acts in a proper fashion," Edna stated, emphatically.

Millicent frowned and looked round, even under the table. "And who is watching? For goodness' sake, Edna, we're past seven decades old—and can barely walk, cannot lift, can barely dress ourselves—so who is noticing? It isn't like we're going down to the barn on Saturday night for the big dance—I say discard convention and live it up right now!"

"Here, here," Miranda sang.

"It is easy for a woman of an improper education and breeding to speak of, but I—an Ivy League graduate, a woman of class and culture—"

"A woman in this place is of no better a class or culture than the least of her companions next to her," Millicent said, gravely, "and the problem with you, Edna, is that you really think you're still on that high horse, but really, Edna, really, you're under it—because you've shrunk too much to even mount it."

"Here, here," Miranda sang.

"Oh, hush, Miranda," Edna said, exasperated, with a flip of her hand toward the old Spanish gal, "you're just like a chirping bird."

"Heh, heh," Miranda sang.

"So," said Edna, addressing Millicent again, "what do you want from life, eh?"

"That!" Millicent cried, pointing to two masked men who were dancing along the upper corridors and soon were skipping down the carpeted steps; and then somehow, some way, in some reconsidered, reconvened parallel universe, they were still skipping and dancing and moving just like young men when they reached Miranda and Millicent, where each of them offered a hand to the lady of their choice, bowed graciously and said, "May I have the honor of this dance, pretty lady?"

Miranda and Millicent were astride an astral projected plane that had recently swung in from the swinging sixties; yet, they somehow managed to offer their hands to the gallant strangers and then were easily and expertly swept up into the strong arms of the two agile men and set about to ballroom dance right across the glossy while-tiled floor as gracefully as a sweet melody carried on the warm breezes of a sweet Summer's song.

But such a splash in such a small pond sent concentric shock circles throughout the nerve center of the cocoon-like place, and the masked marvels seemed intuitively to know this, for presently they were gently depositing their breathless ladies upon their soft cushioned chairs and then fleeing, like dashing young heart-thieves, straight up the stairs and quickly disappearing into the stagnant shadows of the dead hallways.

O, the riot of excitement the masked men generated among the residents was electrifying; O, the outrage among the stringent staff was stupefying, and they were determined to unmask the villains, but failed to do so, for when the rooms were checked and roll call was done, when men were examined carefully throughout the day, no swashbuckler in tights who swings off crystal chandeliers could be counted among them; thus, it was later determined by the managers that the intruders had somehow broken in through an upstairs window and fled back out of it again, as the staff could not consider the impossible alternative answer—that two of their own inmates were indeed the culprits.

With the dynamic building of muscle and bone for the men came too the dynamic building of mind and spirit, and what these men wanted now was not peeping at the receding world through a stingy hole and muttering condemnation through a gaping mouth; no indeed, for their innermost fires had been rekindled and their appetites for life's lusts whetted, and they yearned for love again, for compassion and companionship again, as the memory of woman was still as much alive in them as the memory of their muscular youth.

Sweet Millicent, Gilbert desired, and sweet Miranda, Manny fancied, and the two men commenced to court them, much as the men did in days of old, coyly at first, so no good woman would have sensed even the slightest alteration in her fragile heart by the amount of time the men were present near them, nor even the words the men said that altered the silky web inside their cautious minds that filtered out any undue or deceptive words, any suave vowels and consonant clusters that would innocently penetrate this intricate barrier and set up shop and await the arrival of its expertly stressed brother tones and sister syllables that would soon pass harmlessly through the now-cut web and accumulate with its growing relations to create a ticking monolith that would eventually explode at the proper time and proper place and thus make the web inaccessible to the woman—and she would not even know of its depletion, thus rendering her a slave to her new lord and master: love. This was the way of men to break down their nemesis—suspicion and doubt—within women, and it could not be avoided.

Presently, the men won over their ladyloves, but the prospect of a bright future, as the ladies saw it, was dim, and so, not be to be deliberated upon; for, the women secretly agreed, in old age, love becomes words only, and words only are not enough; and so, in this way, they capitulated to their weakened bodies and perceived the men as charming and silly dreamers, who talked of past glories and invoked the impossible-to-behold glories of today.

It was early Spring, early rejuvenating Spring, early-tapestry, multi-colored-sky Spring, when the youthful buds bloom and release their fragrant aroma into the fresh, warm air, and birds wed and build nests and the world awakens from the awful eclipse of Winter's icy mistress, when Margaret came dancing into the retirement home, pirouetting across the dull carpet and bounding up the stairs like a schoolgirl.

"I have met a man," she said, excitedly, upon entering the room of Gilbert.

"Fabulous!" he said.

"Wonderful!" Manny said.

"He thinks I am young—O, the blessed fool!"

"Why, you are!" Gilbert said, hugging her.

"We all are!" Manny said, hugging her.

"O, I love you both, I really do," she said, wiping away her joyous tears, and then said as she sat next to her two handsome suitors, "but when do we tell the others?"

"Today," Gilbert said, "and today, we leave!"

"Today," Manny said.

"Today, we live again!" Margaret cried, and hugged them again, but then she grew pensive, and said, somberly, "but who will believe you?"

Gilbert smiled, and taking her hands, said, softly, "Those who would know the Truth, always, anywhere, any time, the eternal Truth of what is—the laws of reason and reality, and common sense."

"And common sense isn't so common," Manny said, slyly.

Margaret smiled and said, "Always the witticisms—but it is who you are, and has served you well," and knitting her thin brows, turned toward Gilbert, "and those above and below us, betwixt and between us, they will either recognize the Truth or not, because of who they are, and no matter what we say or do, there is nothing we can do to change that, even though we must try—this much Mr. Wyatt taught us."

There was a mild celebration of something going on downstairs in the recreation room, always a celebration of this or that, and often for no conceivable reason, for the residents needed to celebrate the simple act of waking up and being alive, thought the staff; as it was, everyone was in attendance at this gala, at least everyone who was lucid and physically able to attend.

Gilbert, on the right side of Margaret, and his arm through hers, and Manny, on the left side of Margaret, and his arm through hers, descended the stairs in a rainbow cloud of elegance and old-world style; and what were they dressed in to present such a marvelous display of bravado and supreme confidence? But the fine accruements of vigor and strength that glowed like burning embers all about them.

The three friends stood in the presence of the stunned populace, a populace whose mental capacities to understand this arcane vision around them was temporarily annihilated.

"My friends," Gilbert began, and lifting up his sweat shirt, he revealed a physique hitherto unknown inside the high walls of this slow-moving hearse, a body ripped with muscles and bulging with strength and decorated with a powerful, lean, hard body that seemed the exclusive owner-ship of the young and healthy. Manny did the same, reveal-ing firm arms and a cut chest and trim waist and thick thighs, and a splash of certitude and defiance emblazoned upon his proud countenance.

And, O, Margaret, that still ostentatious show girl, threw off her black cape to present a finely shaped, girlish figure that had not visited her body in decades.

And then the show began!

Gilbert proceeded to perform handstand push-ups, and Manny lifted Margaret into the air as if she were no more than a puffy cumulus cloud, and she proceeded to dance with astonishing grace and agility across the floor; Gilbert and Manny leaped to the ground and knocked off fifty push-ups apiece, and then leaped up and lifted up previously impos-sible-to-lift objects around them; and when the live theater was over, and the staff of the penal colony had admonished the trio that they were setting a bad example for the rest of the populace, Gilbert reached into his pocket and withdrew a white rose and tossed it into the shocked populace, and then spoke, his voice aflame with ardor.

"What you see before you, you can have, too; it is no miracle, it is only an awakening of your dead and buried youth, and it can be yours again if you really want it," and he reached out his hand, "but you really have to believe it can be yours again and the magic will happen!"

"It's a trick," Miss Vickers cried, vexed beyond reason that someone had accomplished what she said was physically impossible, "you're on steroids; you've had surgery—oh, it's horrible, so unnatural!"

Gilbert laughed, and threw back his head. "It's life! Life!" he shouted, and as he approached them as a former fellow slave now, he remembered the cherished words of Mr. Wyatt, and his tone became nearly frantic with imploring, and overwhelming with generosity of hope, and honesty. "My friends, I tell you these things because I know who you are and how you long to be free of frail bodies that imprison you; you can become like us—free again; free to be alive again—it is your inheritance, your birthright, your destiny!"

"You're frightening the chil—these people," Miss Vickers spat.

"O, is it possible," Millicent asked, nearly sobbing, "it seems so extraordinary that it seems impossible."

Gilbert knelt down next to her and held her hands, and his voice was soft and reassuring. "No, Millicent Hargrove, no, it can be yours again if you truly believe and want it."

"No, it's all a lie," Miss Vickers shouted, "you can't promise her such things again—it's not right to promise her a future she will never have."

"Are we impossible?" Manny cried.

"Yes, yes, you are," she returned, "you're drug users, victims of surgery—false messiahs; don't listen to them, folks, they're not real."

"Who will join us and regain all your yesterdays?" Margaret cried out, pumping her hands on high, and then she said, with great force, "Don't you know that you are constantly growing a new body—that's right, a new body—because your cells die and are replaced by new ones, and it is exercise that will give you stronger and healthier cells instead of the weak and decaying ones you have right now—it is exercise that is the magic pill, it is exercise and eating the way Nature intended you to that will bring back your youth," and her voice was pleading now, "and you can have it if only you will make that first step!"

It is an incontrovertible fact that when a revolutionary thought comes into existence and rips a hole in the ordinary fabric of the space-time continuum, there have always been and always will be those who have determined themselves as saviors of the fabric and will quickly act to stitch it back together again, lest their fellow travelers fall through the hole and venture into the realm of the unthinkable and the impossible, where all things are thinkable and possible.

The manager and the assistant manager of the home, in tow with their lessers, descended upon the three friends and ordered the two men back into their rooms.

Gilbert and Manny paid them no heed, while Margaret smiled and winked at them.

"This is a place of segregation," Gilbert cried, and reached out his hands to his fellow captives; "who will come now and free themselves from this slow death?"

The administration threatened to call the authorities for this disruption, and when their antagonists rebuked them, they did just that.

The three friends, sorrow their newest companion, turned and walked back toward the exit, knowing that they would never return to this human ruin of rust and decay, for Margaret had cleverly planned the slow evacuation of the boys' things.

They neared the door, and once more Gilbert reached out his hands, and then shouted, "You can have Freedom from what does not have to be—feel it in your soul, my friends, feel it inside your youthful soul; you know that to die slowly is to accept death slowly—you accept it, it is you who allows it to stay, it is you who allows your youth to drain away from you, it is you who drives it away with every passing second by not listening to its dying words and not watching its dying form before your very heart and mind and soul: it wants to live, and only you can bring it life again."

The response was a dreaded silence, but an expected silence in an institution where devolution in intellectual thought built up in its entrails like cement, like a corrosive sludge of bad ideas and bad motives and bad outcomes that clogged every operating mechanism so thoroughly that the entire system barely moved and moved blindly.

But then there always seems to be one hearty soul who seems to survive and somehow peep its effulgent eyes through the philosophical gunk.

"Wait for me," Millicent cried, standing up and walking with her cane toward them, and then fell into Gilbert's strong arms, where she wept like one reborn; and lo, too came Miranda, and fell into the capable arms of Manny, where she too wept like one reborn; and lo, the five friends retired into the brand-new, mind-and-body-establishing, new birthing Spring, reentering the birth canal and walking past the sloth-filled chamber wherein their brethren had parked their worn-out bodies to await a tortuous, slowly dissembling, molecule-by-molecule death, where slowly—like forager ants tearing apart a stinking carcass flesh by bone by hair—they were consumed, and even willing to submit to the encroaching black radiance of disease spreading over them like an acid ooze, draining their life-force, sucking their life energies; and they did not seem to mind, but our five friends minded, very much they minded, for as they gained momentum together and settled down together and lifted up their feet higher and higher and their forward locomotion became even more powerful and confident, they stepped over the debris of those who had too easily capitulated, stepping higher and clearer, and bounding then, fairly leaping over their own discarded, worn-out flesh, and moving on toward the high citadel whereupon the vital Tree of Life resided, and the sublime song of the silver spheres played, where ebullient life flowed freely and offered its splendid self to any who partook of its free gift of robust energy; yea, they had returned to the world of the living, and their once tired old eyes became open and sparkled as they beheld what they had not seen for so long—life!

-Finis-

# Reunion

**M**rs. Carlisle was sitting at her black steel desk and analyzing the results of the latest test she had administered when a nearly imperceptible smile came to her face and then quickly faded away. "Hmm," she murmured, pleased. "Hello, Corrine."

"Oh, how did you know?" exclaimed the young woman, who now sat in the back row of the classroom.

Mrs. Carlisle did not look up from her work when she said, softly, "You always slid in under the radar," and she paused, "just before the bell," and she delayed the completion of her thought once more, "and quietly, until you sat down hard purposely, to announce that once again, you had made it."

"A habit engraved upon my mind," she said, smiling as she remembered the ruse.

"Yes," Mrs. Carlisle murmured, turning over another group of papers, "the continuing history of the back-row girls."

"But, Mrs. Carlisle, how did you know?"

"Because," she said, and looking up with great warmth and joy, "it is time." Her long red hair fell lightly upon her shoulders.

The special bond that once had been built between them was still there. The Teacher arose and the young woman arose and both of them walked toward each other and soon were in a loving embrace.

"How are you, Corrine?"

Corrine was bathed in the golden sunshine of blessed friendship, but she wore the emblem of sorrow and grief when she said, "Fine," and then smiled through burnt sins and dark betrayals, her face a radiant white diamond sunk into an oozing tar pit, "am I acting now, Coach?"

Mrs. Carlisle smiled. "You're here, now."

Corrine looked around the classroom, smiling at the wonderful memories evoked by the colorful images on the walls, and said, wistfully, "Study the great actresses of the past if you want to be a great actress of the present."

"You remembered," Mrs. Carlisle said, nodding in admiration.

"Of course," she said, and pointing to her head and then to her heart, her voice became filled with affection, "your lessons guide me still."

Mrs. Carlisle searched the beaten and worn but still youthful countenance of her former pupil.

"Beautiful locket, Corrine — thank you again."

Corrine smiled, thinking of the South Sea island she had been on during her last movie shoot. "But my letter, well, it is better left unread..." She hunched her slender shoulders. Mrs. Carlisle said nothing, but waited for the affliction of Corrine's heart to arise. A slow mist of pious tears began to well up in her eyes as she spoke words that dropped like broken glass from the delicate standard-bearers of human indulgences, shame and humiliation. "Well, that last picture," and she paused again, looking round, biting her full, sensual lips, "I lost myself, you see, and I began to do things that were unrecognizable to myself." Once the transgressions were admitted from the archive of her despoiled memory, she could no longer hold back her true emotions. She looked to her Teacher once more, as if in her mentor lay virtues that were steadfast and true and easily assimilated into her own soul. "Oh, Marie, you were right…" Guilt flowed out of her like melting ice in spring.

Marie walked up to her and held her and stroked her amber-colored head of hair as it lay on her shoulder.

"You told us," she sobbed, "you warned all of us, you told us what would happen, you knew, you knew what we would do and still I did nothing…"

Corrine wept her grievous sorrows long and hard as Marie held her long and softly, and when Corrine's surface woes—that is, the woes that were merely the scabs and scales of the deep breach in her heart—came out and unclogged her mind, she was able to speak once more.

"I remember," she began, wiping her brilliant azure eyes with a tissue, "just as if it were yesterday—you said," and standing up straight, she proffered an affectionate and fair representation of her mentor—this talent of mimicry being essential for any good actress—in the passion of a true pedagogue. "'My students, my poor, star-struck students, I envy your talent, yet fear for your immortal soul; you approach the illusion of stardom with a dream, and once you're in this dream, you become that illusion; so what do I speak of, dear students? I speak of that singular race of super beings—we render them mere celebrities; the ancients called them the gods—whose culture is hitherto unknown to mere humans and cannot be supposed; I speak of the inherent dangers,'" and here she was especially adept at lowering her voice to echo the exact stark growl of a coming augury from one who knew, "'I lead you to slaughter, but I want you to run from it, only because I love you.'" Corrine laughed, and looked with affection at her Teacher. "You told us exactly what was going to happen: the drugs, the alcohol, the parties, the romance—no, the sensual love affairs—and the bad drama, just like you would find on any high school campus." She rose up and walked about the room, looking about and smiling and nodding her head in fond remembrance. "In every corner of this room I still live in my memories," she murmured, and then she smiled and laughed and abruptly bolted out through the door.

Marie went to her desk, took out a small black object, read a message on it, smiled, and then walked leisurely after her.

"Now, I am home," Corrine cried, standing on the wooden floor of the theater, and looking out across the empty chairs, whispered to herself, "and always I will remain here, having invested so much of youth in preparation for my inevitable fall from Mt. Olympus, an act not unexpected by the poets..." She skipped girlishly upon the fading maple wooden floor, throwing her hands about and humming a merry tune; she came round full circle, stopping at the front of the stage, and then hesitated, her face drawn in mystery, and then jumped off it and sank into one of the front-row seats, and smiled, turning as if cameras were around her, and then standing, staring at the stage, threw up her arms and hid her lovely face; she stood, turned round, waved, leaped up to the stage and feigned taking an award of some kind from an imaginary presenter and then, wiping away absent tears, she spoke.

The lights dimmed. Corrine truly smiled now as she began to speak.

"I want to thank the Academy for this Best Actress Oscar," and she held out the weightless solid brass albatross.

"You know, I could thank a hundred people and still miss someone, so I'll keep it simple, as it relates to my heart." She paused here for dramatic effect just as she had truly done on that special night of nights. "I thank the man who was my audience, Tyler, and the woman who taught me what being an actress is, Marie; without them, I am just another girl you wouldn't notice, because I am really nothing special outside of the narrow scope of the camera lens…" She held the empty air award on high, and when the lights came on, she turned round toward Marie and said in earnest, "That's one thing I didn't screw up in the last five years."

Marie walked toward her. "I had girls lined up down the block," she said, laughing and clapping her hands together and then stopping next to her protégée, "but they soon stopped coming once they realized it was you, not me; you can't make a silk purse out of a sow's ear."

Corrine let her head fall to her chest, her thick, long hair falling about her bare, bronze shoulders; she lifted her head, her face entranced in a mask of passion, and then she turned to the bodiless audience. "'Farewell,'" she proceeded, moving slowly in the dimming light, "'what's here? A cup, clos'd in my true love's hand? Poison, I see, hath been his timeless end:—O churl! Drink all, and leave no friendly drop to help me after!—I will kiss they lips; Haply some poison yet doth hang on them, to make me die with a restorative.'" It was the final death scene of the impassionate teenager, Juliet, and truly, truly, Corrine was in her own now; truly she was now in horrible agony, her soul resting upon her freshly cut grave as it opened beneath her; for this was Corrine's treasure, a singular gift conferred upon a few citizens of the world, the ability to assume the identity of another completely different person, while completely and utterly displacing her own unique identity, and then living all of their unique traits naturally, and by doing so, convincing others that she was uniquely that person and no other. This gift cannot be taught, only nurtured.

Corrine waxed bleeding pathos, disgorging her entire human spirit of anguish into the quiet audience below; when the scene finished, she lay crumpled upon the faded, wooden floor as if Juliet, as if one dead, dead to her environs, dead to her worldly concerns—for in the world of theater, the only concern was in the world of the play.

A thunderous applause unfurled from the far back rows. "Bravo!" the strong masculine voice shouted. "Bravo!" again it exclaimed, and louder and more impassioned.

Corrine, still prostrate, looked up, narrowing her eyes. The man, wearing a baseball hat and still clapping, came walking down with a slow gait and a small shuffle and his head down and on his face a small smile. "Encore, encore," he shouted, with hands cupped this time as he looked up.

Her face lit up in ecstasy. "Tyler," she rejoiced, and leaped off the stage and hurled herself into his strong, waiting arms.

Marie, arms folded inside her white cashmere sweater, smiled warmly.

"Oh, Tyler, how did you know I was here?" Corrine cried, as the two of them walked arm in arm toward the stage. "I tried calling you for days but you weren't home."

"A little bird told me," he said, his black face brimming with happiness, "right after Roberta and I returned from vacation."

"Marie," Corrine said, looking up, "you conspirator!"

The two climbed the stone steps to the stage and Marie and Tyler embraced.

"A real homecoming," Corrine said, holding both of their hands now, desperate to suppress her burning pain, "my two best friends with me; this is more than any award could ever give me." She wept with joy.

They sat down on three wooden chairs and talked of old times.

Corrine laughed. "I remember the time when you threw down your mop and scolded me for not properly preparing for the role of Antigone."

Tyler sat upright, proudly. "You have to be dedicated to your craft," he said, seriously, and then smiled warmly, "but of course, you know that now."

"And the time Principal Burton scolded you for staying too long during my rehearsals."

"Well," he said with a tone of conciliation, "the man was just doing his job, I guess."

"Why, Tyler, you've mellowed!" Corrine shrieked with delight. "How wonderful for you! Retirement must agree with you."

Tyler frowned and rubbed his salt-and-pepper goatee. "Roberta has a calming effect on anybody who is with her twenty-four hours a day."

The women laughed at this revelation, as they knew the magnificent temper he possessed.

Tyler held the hands of the girl he had watched over for so long with warmth and love, and then gratitude, a special gratitude that only those who love a person and are loved by that person can convey, diffused across his dark face as he beheld her youth. "Thank you, darling," he murmured, and as he kissed her forehead, she felt the deep longing for what had fallen from her heart these past years.

She smiled, embarrassed. "Oh," she whispered, waving him off, "the money they give to people just because they are good at pretending to be someone they are not…" She had always been embarrassed by the exorbitant amount of wealth freely bestowed upon her for her talents.

"Any problems getting here, darling?" Tyler asked.

"Oh, the tangled web," she began, shaking her head. "Someone, someday, really should write a story about the stealth used by celebrities to get from," and here she picked two points in space and drew an imaginary line between them, "point A to point B."

"But you are here," Marie said.

"Here I am," she returned, nodding, "and yet," and she became melancholy, "in some ways, it's like," and she looked about, "I have never left," and she arose, staring at the many colorful and carefully drawn props, "as if the role of rising starlet to serious actress has been merely another play." She sighed and looked to her mentors. "At least I would like to hope it was; I would give all of it up just to awaken at seventeen again, on this old stage, in this fine theater, with the two of you at my aft and fore," and her thoughts seemed to drift away for some time, but then she continued, "an innocent girl who learned her lessons through fantasizing," and she stared for the longest time at the crimson curtains, remembering her carefree and innocent youth. "Hmm," she finally uttered, "you could make mistakes then, and they were just ordinary mistakes an ordinary girl makes and no one noticed—mistakes people even expected you to make because it was just you growing up, and it was just expected, and of course you were forgiven, that was easy," and she looked briefly at her audience, "indiscretions of youth," and she turned her head away, her slender arms wrapped around her voluptuous figure, her face ebullient with enthusiasm as she looked upward. "O, to be full of youthful hope and naivety about the adult world, the world of reality," but her arms fell at her sides, "but the purity of youth is corrupted by this aggressive, amoral real world; if I only had yesterday to begin anew..." She slowly took residence in an old brown rocking chair. She smiled. "I own cars that a Teacher or Custodian could never even buy, and a house, well, a house with the finest furniture," but she was stroking the faded handles of the rocker, "yet, this rocking chair is more comfortable, and means more to me," she turned abruptly to her mentors; "I dream about this rocking chair!" She saw their small smiles. "Oh, I do! I dream about this place," she continued, gesturing about excitedly, and then pointed to them, "and about both of you, of course; I dream—it's funny how the mind works...but I may be on a set in Madrid or at a party in Rome or in the midst of old ruins or great wealth, and yet," and her words developed an authentic longing, "I dream of this, and this place..." There were fresh fumes of regret mixed in her hot breath, black ashes of dead fires falling from her eyes; her internal fire was exhausted, and from her salty pores exuded tiny fragments of her dying heart that landed lightly upon the dusty floor to form a black death wreath. She was wanting to collapse into a curled heap as her mind was stricken with grief, as her body was flung into purgatory, a mindless, shapeless lump of beautiful, tanned flesh that had burned up too quickly as it flew too close and too soon near the bright sun.

She was pulling her hands through her lush honey-colored hair, and tears welled up in her scintillating sapphire orbs, which were set in a rich, snow-white border. "I am home, I know I am," she whispered, up out of the chair now and feeling the folds of the thick curtains, "and now that I am here, and not there, I can't imagine ever being there ever again; but when I am there, I try hard—very hard—to imagine that I was here," and she turned toward her elders, shaking her head, "but I cannot, I just cannot do it, and I don't really know why," and now she openly wept. "I tried, I really tried to pretend I was here, an Innocent again, not who I was, what I had become—a party girl, an alcoholic, a drug user, a fool for any handsome man who was married or—no, I am an adulterer, too, shameless and cruel and not at all worried about the consequences of those around her..." She gulped, choking back her sorrow. "O Marie, O Tyler, I tried to be with you again, but this girl," and she violently clutched her head with her hands, "this now rich and spoiled girl kept getting in the way; and O Marie, when I was there, I didn't want to come back, I didn't want to, really—it would have been like asking me if I no longer wished to be young, or alive—as if it was my right to do what I was doing and no one could tell me otherwise—but now that I am back, I don't want to go back there, ever again, not back to that dark cell where you never even see what imprisons you because you are too busy creating your own prison bars; but, I know, I just know I do not have the strength to stay away," and she closed her eyes; "even now I feel the call of the wild, to go back, back into that maelstrom that people like me create but cannot see until we willfully leave it and condemn it." She trembled, her hot breath coming in short gasps. "What am I to do? I am like a trapped animal who is now free to roam the good earth but seeks to go back into the cage because in there I am somebody—as if being out here, I am less than some-body," and she walked away from them, struggling to keep her delicate equanimity. Her voice was strangled with panic, as if she were tiptoeing on greasy marbles. "I have it all, yet nothing that really matters; I have what I always dreamed of, yet it is a dream that crushes me." She listened to her dead words, words from the grave, a live grave, a grave dug by her soiled behavior. "I am lost, lost," she murmured, to her dying self, numb now, weak now, broken and shattered, now, "lost." She felt her fragile resolve crumbling. "Lost," she mumbled to herself, forgetting where she was, "lost, lost to myself, no good to anybody, dead, dead lost," and she talked her body down to the floor, "twenty-three, and dead to the world…" She felt the force of her words cut the sinew in her muscle and crumble the structure of her bones as she fell to her knees, with her flushed face, wet with hot tears, in her hands. "Who am I, what I have become…" She wept bitterly, and lay down, curled up to fit in her living grave.

\* \* \* \* \*

There she lay, a delicate wisp of a woman, a fading chrysanthemum wilting under the intense heat of a blasting furnace.

"Encore, encore," Tyler shouted, stern-faced, clapping sharply, not once looking at Marie, but only at the crumpled heroine.

Now, just as an extinguished volcano that sits cold and dried of its fiery juices and a burnt candle that sits mired in its own waxy broth are expected to follow the proper protocol and stay in the recesses of sleep, so too Corrine, seemingly extinguished by the terrible debt of self-guilt pressing down upon her, should have stayed down for a standard amount of time.

Alas, she lifted her head, her face covered by her long hair, and looked askance at her audience, her naked face shaved of sorrow.

"The phoenix arises," Tyler said, smiling now, and then laughed as he rocked back in his chair and slapped his wrinkled old hands together in a loud bang.

"How can you laugh?" Corrine weakly protested, rolling over onto her back and staring up at the vaulted ceiling and intricate railing systems and catwalk.

"You forget, little girl, I've known you since you were thirteen years young, a smart-aleck little pistol who knew the world was at her feet if she just smiled," he nearly sang, and here he bore a smile born from wisdom.

"And that means I can't suffer?" she said, sniffing and rubbing her moist eyes.

His voice mellowed now, splintering his coarse tone. "No, sweetheart, it just means I know you, and you wouldn't be so easily knocked down."

She unconsciously nodded. "True, true," she mumbled, and then frowned, "but I do feel terrible."

"Oh, I am sure you do," he said, and stood up and walked slowly over to her and bent down next to her. "Corrine," he whispered, lovingly, "you fell by yourself, you've got to get up by yourself—you can't repair a hole in a wall with more material than you lost."

She smiled in affection, and then reached up her hand to his and grasped it, strongly. "I missed you," she whispered, and began to weep again but aborted it; she sat up, still clutching his hand as he sat down on another brown wooden chair. She looked up at him demurely. "Tyler, how could I behave so poorly after all you and Marie taught me?"

"It's part of growing up, youngster," he said, soothingly; "we can teach you and you can listen but once you're in that ring, well, you know how many times I said that I wouldn't be there..."

"...To hold my hand when times were hard..." She laughed, swinging her hand in his. "I remember once, when you said, 'Little girl, do you think you'll go into a job interview and have the employer ask you a question and then turn around and ask, "well, Tyler, what should I say?"" He smiled at the recollection, and then watched her get up and skip around the room and finally stop at a painted wall scene of verdant meadows and silver lakes and crimson skies. "Tomorrow I go back, and tomorrow I return to my own vomit." She quickly turned toward Marie. "How do I know I am not really a sow's ear and will never be a silk purse, that I am just my mother—a drunken prostitute—but a rich and famous one? I mean, what is the difference—really?" She shook her head and said with conviction, "But you are my family, and yet both of you are so good and kind; but does good and kind last in my new world? What if it simply doesn't belong there; then what do I do? It is what I want, yet if I have it I will gain the world but lose my soul; O Marie, you admonished me of the inherent dangers, but how can I not become so absorbed? The movie business is all about fantasy—it isn't real, none of it—and to stay in it, I have to deny the real world and be swallowed whole by this... leviathan."

Marie stood up. "You're not them, Corrine, you're you; you may look like them and act like them, and you may even have been seduced by them, but in the end, you'll always be you, which is still a bigger part of us, and never even a small part of them."

"I wish I knew that for sure," she returned, clutching her breasts, "in here; but you don't know what it's like there, it's like a child who has never had candy and has always dreamed of delicious candy and then one day finds herself living in candy land and then being told to never eat any of the sweets there."

"You're not a child," Marie scolded her, "so quit thinking like one; you're an adult who has to make adult decisions that affect other people. You have a great responsibility, and you accept it, or perish."

Corrine, ashamed, looked away to the brilliant hues on the wooden prop wall, and whispered, longingly, "Life here was so simple," and then she looked down. "How can things go bad so quickly?" And then she turned toward Marie and said wistfully, "You know, no one ever talks to me like that anymore, not ever, really…"

"Sit down, young lady," Tyler said firmly, and pulled out the three wooden chairs to form a semicircle, and all of the three players in this human drama sat down. "Tell us all about those people who have betrayed you."

Corrine trembled, breathing the debris of smashed acquaintances and the ashes of dead friendships. "Everyone—including myself," but she said it as if she were a child, not at all like the strong archetypal female she portrayed in film and on the stage, not at all like the mature, witty, intelligent actress who was one of the most photographed women in the world.

It was Tyler's time for speeches, a father's sage advice to his wayward daughter. "And what are the most important things in life?"

She smiled, not from here, but from there, a faraway, long-ago, impossibly too-long-ago-to-be-imagined special place. "Faith and family, loving and helping each other, and health, and everything else is just incidental."

"Spoken by rote, daughter; you didn't believe a word of it." He looked at Marie. "Mother, how would you say her acting was on that line?"

Marie spoke with sincerity. "I rate her as a freshman, with absolutely no credulity."

"How do you plead, young lady?" Tyler asked, feigning gravity.

"Guilty," Corrine answered, throwing up her hands.

Spontaneity swept them all up into a hearty laugh.

"Oh," Corinne finally said, looking at both of them, "I really don't want to go back." She sobered up quickly. "Marie, it's just like you said it would be: it is like a narcotic."

"And you're smart enough to know it, and step away."

"And if I go back, I'll become the same fool." Desperate tears began to pool in her luminous eyes. "But if I do go back, I want to be ready this time; O Marie, O Tyler, it is my life, I do love it so, but it will kill me, I know it will; O, what do I do, what do I do…" And her tears came as she sat still, her heart bare and dying for solace.

Tyler was soft in his tone now, loving in his intent, his calming words breathing life into her wounded heart. "You tell your Father and Mother what you want, daughter; we'll be there for you."

"I just want to be happy again, like I was here, and I don't know how to be happy there, and I know I have to be there, or I am lost."

"So, don't go back." He looked at her disturbed countenance. "Sweetheart, you need to do what makes you happy, even if that means living in an apartment and teaching children how to make-believe all day; success isn't measured by who you are in society, it's who you are with people; it's what you do for human beings that count," and he smiled warmly then; "a heart is not judged by how much you love, but how much you are loved by others."

"The Wizard," Corrine said, sniffing and wiping away her tears with a white tissue given to her by Marie.

"Best advice in the whole world," Tyler said, smiling briefly, holding her hand again.

"Tell us what you want, Corinne," Marie said, softly; "you're the only one who knows what your heart needs to heal."

She nodded. "Yes, I know, I know what to do; I need to go away, to step back and see who I was and who I am, now; I need to be a person, part of the world, doing universal acts that make people, anywhere, happy—and real." She looked at them, tears streaming down her beautiful, rosy-red, full cheeks. "I need to cleanse my heart of too much misery and pain, too much sin…" But she wept so that she could no longer speak.

"Don't," Marie said, harshly, "don't start with that."

Shock crept up through her face. "What?"

"You came in here reciting all the axioms and sagacity we pounded into your stubborn brain, and now you seem to have forgotten who we are."

"Marie," she pleaded, "I don't know what you mean…"

"She doesn't know, does she, Father," Marie said, incredulous, turning toward Tyler.

He was desperately silent, broodingly silent for too long, and when he spoke, it was with calm and castigation. "She thinks, Mother," he began, with hard words, "we're talk-show hosts."

Her face blanched, and she froze, her tears dead on her hot cheeks, her faded memory, once sunken, now resurrected and evincing a bloody organ spewing uncomfortable truths; yes, she knew exactly what they meant. Marie had forever lampooned drug-addicted, alcohol-drinking, pill-popping, silly actors and actresses who were ubiquitous on talk shows, crying their sad little party-boozing, syrupy stories of self-destruction and then proclaiming they had rediscovered themselves and cast away the liquid, white-powdered, paper-rolled dynamite for the newest elixir fad—be it yoga that rejuvenated them or a private guru or a powerful new book or miscellaneous philosophies from esoteric faraway lands or trips to the land of the oppressed little people, or a magical lover, a new faith, or just the sweet ambrosial air inhaled deeply while in the mellow bosom of Nature's green harvest. Did the origins of these supposed epiphanies ever matter, Marie had remarked often, for "The little fools are still on their funeral procession; they're just on a small detour around the widening pit."

Corrine trembled in the wake of this shuddering memory. Her eyes were wide, her small nostrils flaring, her lips palpitating. "Do you think this is a farce?"

"Your heart would seek permanent residency in solace," Marie said.

Corinne, angry now, stood up. "What do you want me to do, join a nunnery?"

Her adoptive parents sat still, waiting patiently for her first mortal death, waiting for every piece of her glittering new skin of fame to drop off.

"Acting is my life," she remonstrated; "I just need to get my head together."

Tyler burst out with uproarious laughter, slapping his blue-jean-covered knees. "Girl, if I had a quarter for every time I heard a celebrity say that—heh, heh, heh…"

Indignation propelled her up and pushed her lithe form past both of them and to jump off the wooden stage and to the carpet and to run straight up the aisles and out the double doors.

Marie stood up, walked over to the refrigerator, tossed a bottle of spring water to Tyler, and said, calmly, "Do you remember when you were twenty-three?" and smiled fondly.

"My gosh, everything set me off; I was so passionate about every injustice."

He sipped the cool water. "It is interesting, Marie; I get even more incensed by injustice now, but I'm slower on the trigger about it."

She smiled again. "Half an hour, perhaps?"

"Twenty minutes, and she'll come back as shy as a thirteen-year-old school girl."

They both laughed.

\* \* \* \* \*

She sat in her inglorious black-sedan-incognito car she drove whenever the stresses of life became too much and began to encroach upon her sanity; she gazed into the flip-down mirror and saw the lush, rich brown complexion of her clear face, the naturally full lips, the long, naturally thick amber eyelashes, the arching slender eyebrows, the perfectly formed nose, the lambent burst from her lustrous blue eyes that were set within an incandescent white lake; she saw her face, her sweet face, her adorable face as fresh as a blooming red rose in the early dewy morning and lusted after by human-swine photographers the world over, and kissed by too many men the world over, too—and she did not recognize herself, at all.

She wept.

Now, she saw herself, recognizing herself only in pain.

Twenty-five minutes hence, she crept in the dark toward the auditorium, timidly opened the doors and then coyly walked in.

"It's a meat factory."

Marie and Tyler, conversing, stopped, and looked down the aisles at her.

"All the executives care about is money; it's not art, it's lucre, dirty filthy lucre," she said, and held up her hands as she began to walk, for her words had broken the invisible barrier between them. "I know, I know, I knew it was just a business before I began my journey." She halted at the stage floor. "But does all of it have to be just business? I mean, there are good men and women who care about the craft of film-making, but they're fragile flowers in a garden of virulent weeds." She easily leaped up to the stage. "One of the most famous—infamous—actresses in the world, throwing a fit," she said, in disgust, and embraced Marie and Tyler. "People," she said, sitting down next to them, "actually think we don't have the same biology as the rest of humanity."

Marie smiled, and held Corinne's hand. "Tell us what you want, darling."

She smiled a smile of melancholy strain. "I want peace in my heart and soul," she began, clutching her chest, "away from the mechanical beast, before all of it ends and they write sordid books about another fallen star, before I embarrass myself on screen and off, and expose more of myself than the world needs to know; before," and she hung her head low and then looked up, "before I forget who I used to be, before I forget the way back," and she wept, "before I forget the way back to both of you," and she fell into Marie's comforting arms. "I need to go away, far away," she sobbed, "far away so I can see where I am in the world, so far away that I don't care or remember about who or what I was there." She turned toward Tyler. "I need to find me, and then I'll be fine; isn't that right, Tyler? Didn't you always say that?"

He tenderly stroked her forehead. "Yes, sweetheart."

"Well, I am ready to go away, because being who I am now isn't worth all the money in the whole wide world."

"That's my girl," Tyler whispered, proudly.

She sat upright. "I'll go away, and if I come back, I come back as I went in, and I will stay that way, and if they don't want her, then I won't stay."

They talked for two more hours, she telling them sordid tales, they listening patiently, and all of them making plans for her future. Then Corrine stood up, kissed them both on their cheeks, and departed.

She came back in twenty minutes later, finding them both still sitting on the wooden chairs, and now staring with parental wisdom at her.

She shook her head, exasperated, and gesturing wildly. "I know what you're thinking: you're thinking that she's going home and she'll feel better now that she thinks she has gone through a total transformation, and that she'll go back to the movies and the parties and then she'll get into another funk and she'll be right back here again and do the catharsis act once more—just like your average, pathetic, boozed-up, drugged-up actress."

Marie and Tyler sat, somber faced.

"Well, I won't fail you, I won't; I'll be back, I will, I'll be back in one week, as soon as I put my affairs in order."

But her wise counselors simply stared, conferring judgment upon her shrinking form.

"I will," she cried; "why don't you believe me?"

Tyler rose up, walked over to the edge of the wooden floor, and crouched down close to her, his countenance severe. "When you were thirteen years old, and your mother killed herself after killing your father, you left to live with Marie and you never returned to your old home; child, that's you, when you leave hurt, you leave it then and there; there isn't any wavering with you." His voice softened. "If you aren't really hurting now, then you'll go back and party for a year or two until the hurt returns and then you'll seek refuge again. It's the way you are; heck, it's the way we all are."

Corrine gazed into the dark eyes of the man who had helped raise her after her parents' demise, a man who had counseled her, advised her about boys, helped her with her schoolwork, given her the stable, positive, loving presence of a father in her life—he, Tyler, the school custodian, had given these great yet simple gifts to her.

"I know," she responded, with downcast eyes.

But he lifted up her chin. "Don't ever despair when you're with family."

She smiled, that special sort of smile only a daughter can give to caring parents, which speaks of trust and love.

He stood up as Marie came to rest at his side.

She looked up at them, her face playfully inquisitive. "Marie, Tyler, can I go home now?" She flushed with pride as she beheld their joy. "O, let's go," she sang, jumping onto the stage and hugging them. "Tyler, what is it like living in a Mexican village? Come on, come on, you just came back from there—give me details, details…"

All of them were now walking slowly toward the back of the stage.

"Well, little daughter, thanks to your generous donations to the village of Santa Rosita, they now have running water."

"Really? How wonderful! But do they know who I…"

"No, darling, to them, you would be just another gabacho."

O, how all of them laughed then, as only a real family laughs, honestly and lovingly and as one.

-Finis-

# Oblivion

S ometimes events can happen only in certain places, and sometimes events can happen only in certain times, and sometimes these events will happen despite the place and the time. There was an event that occurred in a certain time and in a certain place, and the time it did occur in was perfect and its planners could never have imagined a better place.

It was the age of medical experiments when doctors and scientists were allowed to take people and expose them to conditions that are now defined as too harsh and too perilous and too damaging to the human mind and body. It was the era of injecting people with insidious disease and then watching its effect on them; it was that era—the era of subjecting people to electric shocks and sleep deprivation and caloric starvation and every kind of stimulus to get them to perform just like their brother and sister lab rats; it was the era of psychological testing without borders, without restraints, without checks and balances; and when it was all over and done, and the data recorded and the impact felt, great strides into the secluded, guarded, repressed world of Man had become a little clearer.

But the whole business of physically and mentally injuring volunteers was certainly gone by the time the media woke up and the human rights groups woke up, too; and subsequently, up taller stood the white rats, up taller stood the wooly sheep and up taller stood the furry chimpanzees.

There is one experiment from this bygone generation that has never been published in any reputable journal or magazine, or any ambitious newspaper, simply because it was recognized by even the scientists at the time as being excessively cruel and perhaps even unnecessary, and so they repressed the final data and smothered it and buried it in the deepest black hole imaginable.

* * * * *

The Salton Sea is really just a great, salt-covered depression which is filled with water that broke through its barriers from the Colorado River; it soon became a huge tourist attraction and people from all over came to the Salton Riviera to fish and boat and bird-watch, and even camp and swim and hike; there were even resort towns built, where people played golf, water-skied, and could spend their nights at a glitzy yacht club. There was a young scientist by the name of Stuart Kafka, who was visiting the boundaries of the shore one warm, breezy morning, and he happened to wander over to a small set of ponds that had been built as a bird sanctuary. In the center of each small pond was a patch of dirt upon which sat dozens of screeching Caspian Terns with their snow-white feathers and orange beaks and silly black caps, or dozens of Gull-Billed Terns with their snow-white feathers and stout black beaks and silly black caps on another. He was immediately struck by the fact that the birds never quieted down and that the noise was even deafening to him from his vantage point of fifty yards away. It was then that he hit upon the grand idea and immediately went back to his laboratory to write up the proposal and eagerly submit it to his superior.

It must be remembered that this was the age of unabridged and unsupervised, completely out-of-control scientific experiments that will not and cannot ever happen again in America, when Dr. Wright, Head of the Department of Psychology, said to Stuart in a voice more resembling the noise a man makes when he is being violently beaten upon his person, "Are you out of your mind?"

But Stuart was young and ambitious, and this experiment was impetus for him to simply do and not analyze, as was the case for most of his peers. "Sir, I realize the severity and risks inherent in this proposal, but I believe it will illuminate the vague and unexplored areas we have on human isolation, and quite frankly, sir, with the Cold War and all, we have to be concerned with soldiers and spies being captured and kept in solitary confinement and the effect this has on their mind and whether or not they will break—and even if they do, to determine whose fault it is, and who to punish and who to reward; sir, it might be an important experiment for national security."

It was the also the time when America was fighting the Union of Soviet Socialist Republics in every city and town, heart and mind, and nook and cranny, and when men were being captured by the enemy and their bodies were being assaulted to give pleasure to the captor and their brains were being assaulted to extract valuable information from them; it was the time when the government was very generous with grants to universities who could help the military win that Cold War; and it was also the time when the eldest child of Dr. Wright was in the army.

But still, Dr. Wright was unmoved. "I do not see the merit of this experiment, Stuart; it has no meaning outside of itself—it is as if you have created this test to determine how long a man might endure suffering with no immediate recognizable goal. I must deny this request."

"Dr. Wright," he replied, immediately, as he had rehearsed his response to every conceivable objection, "the goal would be for the man to survive these harsh environs and regain his freedom—that would be the prize."

"Stuart, the man knows he will regain his freedom in a year's time as it is, so he would simply endure suffering for a goal he knows is his, or he will capitulate very early on when he realizes there is no sense in suffering so long for something he might easily win if he merely steps off the island."

"Dr. Wright," Stuart said, in earnest, "what if we do offer the man a prize—say, a hundred-thousand-dollar prize, equal to a prize the precious freedom a prisoner of war might earn if he knew he had only to endure a year in isolation?"

Dr. Wright mused upon this for a long while, and then said, "Yes, that is a possible solution, if you could secure a grant from the government; although I must state for the record that this experiment is too extreme."

The grant was secured, the full experiment was written up by Stuart and submitted to his senior advisors at the university, and readily accepted. But then no volunteer would take the assignment, for no one was willing to accept the inhumane parameters imposed upon them during the test, so Stuart volunteered—because he had a young wife and many bills to pay—despite the vehement protestations of his colleagues at the university; but he was young and ambitious, and thought he would live forever just as he was then.

One week later he was on Bird Island, and here he was to stay for one solid year, unable to leave the thirty-foot-by-twenty-foot patch of brown dirt, clothed only in a beige loin-cloth, and unable to communicate with any human being. Once a night, in the blackest pitch, preferably as the subject was sleeping, he would be visited by a courier, who would be wearing earmuffs and a mouth restraint and a black mask and would shove a small platform filled with food and a bucket of fresh water and containers for waste toward the small isle, and would leave only when the radio-controlled boat had accomplished its mission.

So, on April 3, 1956, on a pleasant Spring morning, Stuart was delivered to this bird sanctuary that was now hidden to the public by a wall of lumber and cement that was fifty yards from him and rising some twenty-five feet high. Thus, he was now the running mouse in the labyrinth, the swimming rat in the vat of water, the germ in the test tube, and he was here to stay for three hundred and sixty-five days with nothing for company but pond water and the awful smell of pond life and the omnipresent Terns.

There were cameras installed in the walls to survey the ponds. The 8 mm film would be changed out by the courier. There was a guard, who patrolled outside of the walled area, to be replaced every eight hours by another guard. Everything was in readiness.

So, there Stuart stood, hands on white hips, inhaling the briny sea breeze and listening to the noisy screeches of the Terns as they flew about him in panic, his pale feet deep in the mush of dirt and bird droppings as he looked around at a world that had suddenly become much smaller and unappetizing; and he was not perplexed, as he reasoned that he would appeal directly to his supremely intellectual mind to approach every day like just any other day while forgetting about the day before. It is in this fortunate way that youth seek to conquer the world through their hearty ambitions.

\* \* \* \* \*

It is the same with all tortures that afflict the human mind. The first drop of water on the forehead seems inconsequential. The first blast of electric shock seems manageable even as it rips a firestorm through your gut. The first lacerating lash of the whip stings but the body stiffens and resolves to endure. The first punch in the face does not devour but only manages to slow you down. But it is erosion that wins the day, and erosion is the key for any small foe to win the long and torturous battle against an overwhelming enemy.

Take a small grain of sand and throw it against a gigantic boulder. The boulder will puff out its rocky chest against the tiny grain and it will bounce away, leaving the boulder to feel superior and impregnable; but the sly grain, even as it lies on the ground before the mighty boulder, knows differently, for on its very physical borders lies the knowledge that it dented a microscopic particle of rock from its victim, and knows that soon, its brother and sister grains shall pick up the fallen sword and continue the onslaught; it is also in this way that a small creature—like the locust, the army ant, even Man—although somewhat insignificant by itself, might amass with its brethren and conquer great obstacles.

It was his first night on Bird Island, and Stuart was attempting to sleep, but the birds would have none of it. The Gull-Billed Terns had naturally resented his human intrusion, fleeing to a nearby island that was inhabited by the much larger Caspian Terns, who let out their raspy "kowk,

kowk" cry as the cousins jostled for position; but when the human lay down to rest and seemed not to move, they came back and camped out again upon their humble home and resumed their wailing "kay-wek, kay-wek" cry.

The deluge of noise penetrated his deep sleep that lay like a dense mist upon the prone human, and he soon awoke; vexed now, he flapped his arms and shouted at the birds, who once again flew away to an island inhabited by the Caspians, but soon finding themselves reproached by their brother and sister birds, they came back to roost upon their own island, once more awakening the human and provoking him to chase them from his new home.

Stuart did not sleep very well that night.

He awoke in the early morning and immediately chased the birds away, and although somewhat tired, he still retained a good amount of energy—as he was still young and able to subtract large amounts of sleep from one night and still not suffer the consequences the next day—and he was pleasantly surprised to find the small flotilla of food and fresh water awaiting him. He ate a delicious breakfast, deposited his waste matter in the second canister, and sat down to contemplate his situation.

"That is one day gone, and I must prepare my mind for the next day, now, where every day will be new, and the old day forgotten," he began, nodding in satisfaction as he looked about his new environs; "it is in this way that the superior man endures such trials."

He was a family man, yet had no family around him; he was a voracious reader, but had no books about him; he cherished a great musical symphony, but there was no music anywhere; yet, there were the incessant family of birds around him, and the living books of birds unfolding about him, and the great musical score of the twittering and screeching birds that echoed off the surrounding walls and placed his senses inside a banging acoustical chamber; but this did not seem to bother him yet, that the lives of birds would now fill his senses as the sights and sounds and smells of his family and friends and colleagues and music had, for he could not yet imagine a world of the birds, for the birds, and by the birds.

* * * * *

He had managed to keep the birds away that day and this seemed to cheer him, and so when night came and the old white hot souls revealed themselves up in the great domed theater of black space, he lay down to rest and determined how he would erase all that he had experienced here and begin anew tomorrow, and imagined the content of his dreams.

"Adele, you would not believe the stink of this place, and the bugs—O, Adele, the bugs are in your senses all day and night; they are truly an obnoxious race," he said, plainly, as if indeed his wife were somehow able to hear him, a two-person play he had carefully written and practiced before he came here, "and the residual droppings of those menacing birds—a stench that seems irreversible, but I will just have to manage it; I have much to tell you, sweetheart, when I get home."

He went to sleep easily that night but soon awoke to the squealing of the original renters of the island. He chased them away. He went back to sleep. They woke him up again. He chased them away again.

In the morning, he was somewhat tired, but the small flotilla was there and so he feasted on a good breakfast and felt stronger and thus convinced himself that the lack of sleep had done nothing to him. By midday, he noticed something unusual. "Adele, I do believe I am sunburned," he said, feeling the reddened tissue on his arms and back and legs, "I had not anticipated that." He dwelt upon this problem for a while and decided that he would smear mud over his body to block out the harmful rays of the sun, and once it was done pronounced it successful, albeit impractical. "The stench is too much for me," he declared.

One of the conditions of the terms of the agreement stated explicitly that he could receive no supplies once he was on the island, and that if he needed medical attention of any kind, he would be forced to terminate the experiment. By the third day, he was fried and baked inside his fleshly raiment. The sun had increased its intensity and his body had decreased its resistance to pain and suffering. He was sleeping less. He was becoming exhausted. His body had severe second-degree burns from the ultraviolet rays sinking into his light skin. Melatonin darkened to shield him from harm but there was simply too much uninterrupted exposure. He became ill. He became feverish. He became delirious.

And so the birds regained their island and refused to yield it back to the prone figure before them, which they excreted waste on and danced on and squawked on, all of them, every last one of them; and big and small Terns, young and old, male and female, flew over him and around him and landed on him and sang their victory song that this home-wrecker was vanquished. Balance was restored in the five island ponds.

The human body seeks equilibrium. It desires radiant health. It wants peace and harmony within its fragile borders. If you burn it, it will peel; if you poke it, it will seal; if you sicken it, it will heal; the human body will unclog the clog and flush out the toxins and liberate the mind from debris if only the brain resident obeys the natural laws that allow rejuvenation. The body can do nothing with things that it does not recognize, like foodstuffs that come from the commingling of artificial ingredients; and so, the body therefore needs the raw, vital juices of Nature to repair, mend, and exhilarate itself, and this the fallen man received every day on the floating vessel good, wholesome food, and good, refreshing drink, and soon, he was up and about and rebutting the running commentary of his importunate roommates.

The sun continued to wage war against his naked skin. "So, mistress, I must wage war against thee," Stuart declared against his blushing nemesis, and after much thought he began to use his utensils to dig into the center of the isle to build a dirt igloo; but he soon found out that he could penetrate only a few feet down before hitting water, and so was forced to abandon this project. "At least I have altered my surroundings, and in this way I might gain an advantage, certainly," he said, looking upward, "over that orange predator in the sky." He proceeded to experiment with the hole, to lie in it, to heap up mounds of dirt on one side and then lie in its fresh impression and see if the mound blocked the sun—which it did only in the morning and late afternoon. "And what good is that, when the sun is at its weakest, and not seeking my destruction. The sun, who would have wondered about you, as you neither reap nor toil, neither help nor hinder us as we live our lives, but now—O Adele, the things you never notice when you live your life in a pumpkin shell."

He could feel the sizzling drops of burning light settling upon his tender skin, and he felt his body heave toward illness again, and again, he found himself lying on the isle, helpless and feeble and slave to his master, the grinning sun; and again, the birds united and celebrated and considered the invader vanquished once more, for they considered him merely another animal, but thus far a rather lucky one, who, unlike other animals they had observed lie down in their death throes and stay down, managed to rise up again. But soon came the cool liquid and the good food and the good fortune of the man having a healthy and strong body and once more he was revived. "Yet how long might I achieve such a miracle," he asked aloud, "before I must quit this humble domicile, and join you, Adele?"

And it had been only ten days thus far on this misbegotten wasteland.

\* \* \* \* \*

He was now covering himself up with the pots and pans during the day as he lay in the mild depression and at least protecting the most damaged parts of his scorched body. He attempted to cover himself with mud again but still was repulsed by the acrid smell. "But this will not do, no, not at all, for I must find a permanent solution." But try as he might he could not deliver himself from the omnipresent beams of light when they alighted directly atop him, and presently he was felled and lay trembling and feverish and quite out of his mind. The birds, considering him down for good this time, settled upon their domesticated home once more and once more began their incessant chuckling and clattering noise.

It is in delirium that sometimes we do what we ought or sometimes manage to do what we dare to muse upon when we are sober; and sometimes, we do things that need to be done but might only be done when we are quite ostensibly insane. In his spinning mind, in his mind that turned and bent off its axis and was thrown into the pointed shafts of light to be burned like so much fluff and mist, he reached out in his reeling madness and clutched one of the birds and rent it asunder and spilled its blood and guts onto the isle, and then declared in a thundering appeal, "Let this be known high and low to your kinsmen that I mean to rule here alone, for I am a jealous master!"

The birds fled.

"I do not know where I am going but I will yet get there," he mumbled, looking at the corpse of the bird, "and of this place I have sounded the blaring trumpets of war; Adele, where are you now, my good wife, where are you, these days..."

When his body no longer despaired and his soul no longer grieved and his mind cleared, his eyes opened and he saw the rotting body of the small Tern, and he stared at it for the longest time, as if wondering how it came to be there, and then he remembered. "It is true I hated thee; you brought no ill will against me, but sought only to live on your ancestral land; forgive me, dear one." He dug a small hole and buried the bird and felt shame. "Surely, it was the illness that brought me to such villainy." He looked at the birds on the other islands and he stood straight up. "I am able to recognize the Terns who live here; how is that possible?" He stared at the isle to his left, and counted four birds there that belonged with him, and to his right, five birds, and behind him, six birds, and in front of him, four birds. "Adele, this is most curious, as normally all birds seem the same to me—ah," he shouted, slapping his upraised hand against the rarified air, "it is not my concern, for my concern is of the unabashed sun, who lords his power over me like a taskmaster; O, unmerciful sun," he shouted, shaking his fisted hand against his silent foe, "I would think thee into a ball of ice to give myself over to one day of rest from thee, and blast the rest of Creation, for they have forsaken me."

It was overcast for two days and Stuart celebrated. It rained warm rain for two days and Stuart cheered. "My strength returns to me, and I return to me," he said now, walking about like a monarch in his lonely Kingdom, but then the heat and sunlight burst through and meddlesome Summer was back. "I will roast like a chicken on a spit," he lamented. He began to think of capitulation. "It is not as if I am a prisoner here, for I can merely walk off this dung heap and into the water and knock down those idiot walls and in an hour's time I will be with my beloved again." He began to envision himself walking away and down the long dirt road and to a phone booth and charging a call to his beautiful wife and hearing her beautiful voice and trying not to cry and telling her how much he loved her and how soon he would be home, and then seeing himself running down the road and having people staring at his nearly naked form as he all the while laughed and smiled and thought only one long, luxurious thought, and that was to be with his young and beautiful Adele and to kiss her madly and wildly and with unbridled passion. This was what he wanted most of all right now and so he moved closer to the edge of the brown dirt and stared directly into the green mulch of the cloudy water and felt himself pulled down toward it. "I crawled the length of hell and found oblivion; I will walk the length of heaven and find life."

And then a small bird landed next to him and shattered his reverie. "Dare you tempt the king?" he shouted, but then his wrath subsided when he saw that it was wounded. "Well, go away, you loathsome bird, go to the fates," he whispered, turning his head and looking at the walls around him, "as I now must." But the weak squeaking of the bird seized his mind and turned his attention toward the pathetic thing and he felt pity for it. "It would be better had you never been born than to die thusly," he declared, shaking his head, "but, even still," and as he walked toward it, the bird struggled to retreat but faded only to the left and then down to the wet ground. "Now, I have you, you rascal!" He inspected the creature and decided that a splint was in order for the busted wing. "You are only a bird, and so whether you live or die is of no consequence to me, but I will at least show your brethren I have a heart; here, now, you silly creature, hold still!" And presently, the wing was bandaged and splinted, and the frightened Tern fluttered about from one side of the isle to the other. "You might as well get used to it: there is no escape, my little friend."

He was sitting and deliberating strategies for blocking the shafts of sunlight when a Tern landed near the wounded bird and immediately began to preen the infant's feathers and cradle it to its white breast. Stuart smiled. "Is it not the same for human mothers?" He recognized this adult female. "I will call you Vivian, and your baby I shall call Scarlett." As he watched the mother and daughter snuggle together, he reached out his hand to stroke them, and he was surprised when the birds did not object to this, but instead cooed. "How is this possible, Adele; are they not wild creatures, possessing an internal mechanism that causes them to flee from human beings and predators? Do they not know that it takes generations to lose their acquired fear of Man? But perhaps these birds are unique in all the world." He smiled, then. "Perhaps I am unique in all the world." But then he laughed heartily. "Adele, you know better, my love! O, Adele, soon, soon!"

Slowly, like scattered drops of rain, the Terns came back to the isle, and then, like a thunderstorm, all of them were there. Stuart stood among them, and they, seemingly unafraid, walked about him, even allowing him to stroke their soft, feathered bodies. "Remarkable, remarkable," he said, sitting down and watching them hop onto his leg and walk up to him to be petted, "an academic paper here, to be sure, but probably not believed; but I believe it." He no longer felt resentment toward their incessant noise. "Although one could not yet call you friend," he said, looking at them, "for now we only tolerate one another."

He actually slept that night.

He awoke to find his delicious cuisine settled on the small island, the food and liquid contents covered and secured; he ate heartily, and after depositing his waste into the waste container, he set about to muse upon the problem of the sun, "Of whom I hate," he often said now as he glanced skyward toward the mocking redder-than-the-reddest-blood orb. On this day, he noticed that there were numerous feathers on the isle, and he picked up several of them and then placed them on his peeling skin and gazed upon the assembling picture; he anxiously took up more feathers and then placed them next to the other feathers and soon he had covered his entire outstretched left arm in this manner. "Eureka!" he shouted. "A cloak for Summer and Winter!" Presently, he had covered both of his arms in the stinking feathers. "But nothing to attach the feathers with—what I wouldn't give for some needle and thread!" It must be remembered that the rules of the contract specifically stated that the subject could receive no instruments to help him survive on the land, and could receive only food and water and a container to deposit his waste. "But I need needle and thread to mend my fine clothes; what is the harm in that?" He had been given a set of pencils and a notebook of paper to record his thoughts during this experiment, and so now he wrote down his request for the needle and thread and sent it on the flotilla device back toward the shore. The next day, the meals came, but no needle and thread. He cursed.

He set to thinking about the problem of adhering the feathers to his tender skin, and that night, he hit upon the idea, and so worked feverishly upon it so that by the morning all was in readiness. "There," he said, shaking his fist at the mighty white hunter in the cerulean sky, "Man outwits thee, you faithless lover!" He had spread a thin layer of mud on his arms and legs and then carefully placed a first layer of feathers inside the stinking mud he now somehow tolerated, and then spread another layer of the brown mud atop that and then another layer of feathers into that, and by doing so, he had covered his arms and legs in stable feathers. He abruptly stood up and shouted, "I am the birdman!" The Terns squawked and screeched their approval.

In a week's time, he had covered all of his skin with feathers. "Oh, what my colleagues must be thinking back at the university," he said, smiling and nodding his head as he stared at the 8 mm cameras around him; "he has lost his mind; but, no, he has gained his mind in order to survive this place. Adele," he mouthed it carefully toward his mechanically audience, "get ready to celebrate in style when I get home!"

He watched with pride and curiosity as the Terns built their nests in dense patches of yellow grass on the shoreline. "One day Adele and I shall too build a nest," he often said with pride during this time, "and soon, you will be proud papas and mamas, as will Adele and I, one day…"

One morning, he awoke and had his usual breakfast, and when he stood up, he felt a deep ache in his back. "Have I suddenly grown old?" He pondered this for a good while and finally reasoned that he needed to start exercising; so, he took to running in place and performing all kinds of calisthenics, such as push-ups and sit-ups. "This is for you, Jack," he said, at the end of every routine; "Adele, you are a good and caring wife—you had me watching him in the morning, and now I understand his philosophy." He thought he was on his way.

He gazed in wonder at the baby birds that came out of the small, speckled eggs and admired how the parents cared for their young. "Is it not with all creatures, great and small?" He watched the other Terns, the Caspian Terns on the other isles, fly away with their young toward the warm lands and waited for his own Gull-Billed Terns to join them, but they did not go. "But you must go, it is your instinct, you can do no other." But the Gull-Billed would not listen to him, and most of them stayed, and only a few flew away with their offspring.

And then Winter came, and with it came the punisher, cold, and its henchman, rain.

"How could I have not foreseen this?" he asked, observing the black clouds assembling over him and sprinkling him with their icy daggers. "I should have stipulated that certain clothes be available to me." He shook his head. "No, no, it would have invalided the experiment—this is no picnic, no vacation; this is purgatory, as is prison, as are prisoner-of-war camps: so too must I experience their every deprivation." He looked upward. "So, rain on me, if you must, I will be here, rain all the day and night, I will still be here; your fellow god, the sun, could not chase me off this isle, and you, O mighty wind and rain and cold, will not achieve it, either; for you are merely Nature, and I mighty Man, and Man is the master of Nature because he can subvert thee."

It certainly rained hard that night, and try as he might, he could not flee from its menacing touch, and he cried and whimpered like a beaten dog, so miserable and vexed was he. He shouted at the rain to stop and pleaded at the cold rain to stop and threatened the merciless pounding rain to stop but stop the rain would not because it merely followed the dictates of Nature and paid no attention to the ranting man. In the morning, he was disheveled and disheartened. "Get me off this floating prison," he shouted, feeling wet and soggy inside his bird cloak, and looking at the dark clouds above and feeling the strong winds and seeing the sprinkling of rain again, he cried, his fisted hands in the air, "Is there no justice?" He looked to the cameras and picked up a handful of dirt and threw it toward them. "You come here and survive this Nature's idle chatter! This guinea pig is through, do you hear me, through!" and he began to walk off the isle, but abruptly abated. He cursed. "Why don't I just leave? Wouldn't a prudent man simply leave? Am I being brave or foolish?" The hard rain resumed and he covered his head with his arms and he squatted down on the soft dirt and began to weep. "Adele, do you weep for me, do you even know what I am going through for us, do you?" he shouted. He wanted her to suffer as he suffered. "How can I go back to you when I know you are sitting comfortably and warmly in front of a fire and sipping hot chocolate, while I slowly die out here?" That night, he had a terrible fever. "Adele, you should be here with me, you should, you are my faithful wife, through sickness and through health," he mumbled, "you should be here with me or it will be no good; how can I go back and hold you when it is only I that has suffered the sting of Nature's mean breath? How can I trust you again unless you appear before me, wanting to be with me during my trial and tribulation?" His body trembled and his mind quaked. "Adele, you ought to be with me until I die, even if it is now; it is your rightful place; would I not do the same for you?"

And no matter what he did or how he did it, no matter how he curled up or turned or which direction he faced, he could not flee from the onslaught of cold and wind and rain that felt as if it were occurring within his wet skull and cold flesh, flushing him from the inside out until even he felt as if his very soul was soggy and drowned.

When upon he awoke in the morning, he found to his amazement that he felt drier than he had recently been, yet could still hear the harsh music of the tiny water musicians as they brought their tiny cargo to bear upon the isle and pond. "Am I home?" he pondered, and as his mind cleared, he beheld a remarkable sight—he was covered by the Terns. He stared up at them and saw that they were sitting quietly and contentedly upon his curled-up body. "What sort of sign is this, that they are doing this weird thing? What mischief do they engage in?" His fever had broken and his mind was clearing. "Is it yet possible that they are doing this thing to protect me—well, you fool, what other purpose is there for this singular act?" He cautiously reached out his hand and petted some of the birds, and they cooed and rubbed their soft, furry white heads against his hand. "Is this Nature, then, unspoiled, before Man corrupted it, where Man and beast can co-exist without fear of each other?" A frown broke his smile into fragments. "But shouldn't all of you be flying south for Winter, eh? I certainly do not want you to stay here for my sake—after all, I am mighty Man, and am able to alter my surroundings—ha!"

The obnoxious bugs were gone and the obnoxious sun was dethroned and the obnoxious birds were now his friends and so now he could manage the ill-tempered Winter. He had mastered it all and he still had his mind and body and spirit. So, when he stood up in his multilayered bird cloak of white feathers, which often needed layers of fresh mud to adhere to his skin, and beheld the ponds around him and knew the cold could not bite him and the rain could not wet him, he felt invincible and unalterable. "Adele, there is nothing left for me to conquer but time."

He would now spend most of his day playing and caring for the birds, and teaching them about all manners of life, and people, places and things. "D'Artagnan, Athos, Aramis—and Porthos, too?" he said, feigning a stern countenance, for it is true he was much too tenderhearted now to truly scold them, "my dear fellows, do not jostle your beloved sisters, you must always remember to act like respectful gentlemen; so, apologize to your beloved sisters: Aphrodite, Antigone, Athena, and Atlanta—the four 'A's,' I call them—now, isn't it better to be nice? We are learning! How wonderful!" He tended to their wounds and scolded them for fighting with each other and sent them flying through the air so they might return to his outstretched arm. He teased them because they had lost their silly black caps and called them "baldy." He no longer smelled their awful stench or the stench of their droppings or the stench of the pond.

But in the very early golden-crowned dawn, he would say, excitedly, "Story Time Theater," and watch in delight as the birds, as if sensing the fluctuation of tone and pitch in his voice, amassed themselves in front of him, on him, and even atop him. "Now, sit still, my little darlings," he began one cool morning, wide-eyed, and whispering in the language of special treats for obedient children, "our newest story is about to begin—what's this, eh? Heathcliff and Catherine, for shame—don't shove each other, remember your heritage and breeding; and Hero and Leander, no pecking each other! Have some dignity! Well, are we all ready? By special demand, another story from that wonderful Danish author, Hans Christian Andersen—'The Ugly Duckling'! Yes, yes, I know, it is your favorite, and now here it is!" And he would begin the careful narration of it, infusing the life-force of every character into his animated face: now the mean ducks, now the arrogant cat, now the ridiculous hen, now the beautiful swan; and when he had finished, "Who would have believed that so simple a bird could have so many adventures, and have such a noble future—and why not all of you? Eh? What is that? Another, another tale, you say?" and he cupped his ear as they moved excitedly about. "Your wish is my command; so, today, we hear the story of," and he paused, and said, with mirth splashed across his countenance, "drum roll, please," and beat his hands upon his thighs, and then exclaimed, "that wonderful English Folk Tale, 'Henny Penny'!" and he laughed as he watched the birds chirp and flutter about. "Henny Penny, that silly knucklehead who nearly caused a riot because she was ignorant of science—a lesson to be learned, little ones."

And after he had narrated an Aesop Fable, "The Goose that Laid the Golden Eggs," he excused them for recess, watched with joy as they flew about the private sanctuary, and ate to their heart's content; and when they returned, he calmed them again, and began what he called School Days.

"Today, my little scholars, we examine one of your favorites: physics, and for this lesson, we examine how you are able to fly; it is called the Bernoulli Principle—but ah, you do not need to know that; now—what's this? Jason and Perseus, stop that tomfoolery, and remember your destiny—and you there, Cleopatra, is that the way a proper princess behaves, pinching her friends? I think not; so, heads up, wings folded, eyes and ears open; now, to open with a demonstration—you, there, Icarus, go fly," and he lifted up the small fellow and gently threw him into the air, and watched him with pride as he circled about, "remember what Daedalus told you—not too close to the sun," he said with a smile and a hearty laugh, and then watched with pleasure as the master aviator landed on his outstretched hand. So it went this day, and tomorrow, a lecture on chemistry, and generally followed by biology, geology, and after that, astronomy. Now, after this, he excused them for recess, watched with joy as they flew about the private sanctuary, and ate to their heart's content; and when they returned, he calmed them again, and began what he called Music under the Stars.

On this day, once they were sitting quietly before, around and on him, he began thusly. "Did you know, my little friends, we are all—all of us—that's right, I am even talking about you, Charlemagne," he sang, and wearing a silly expression, patted him on his ever-moving head, "and you too, Queen of Sheba," and patted her on her ever-moving head, and spreading out his great feathered arms, "all of us are musical creatures," and then whistled a tune so merry that his appreciate audience reciprocated in kind. "See what I mean? Yes, I have complete confidence that, if given human thought, you could be the finest composers of the day, creating the finest symphonies!" He held out his arms, and the birds soon covered them. "Sing, sing, my little darlings, as only you can, in perfect harmony!" And they proceeded to tweet in a melodic choir. "Excellent! Bravo!" After carefully letting down his arms, and watching them return to their original places, he clapped, and cried, "Encore! Encore!" and moving his arms around in a special pattern, the birds recognized it as a signal to sing once again, to which he moved his hands about, as if an air baton in hand. "Beautiful! Magnifique!"

And when this was done and celebrated, he commenced with the Musician of the Day.

"Ludwig van Beethoven was a great composer of classical music—perhaps he aspired to be a bird, and why not, he knows they are Nature's finest living symphony! A round of applause for yourselves!" and as he applauded, the Terns began to be excited, and chirped loudly. "Well, he must have listened carefully, for in his later years—try not to cry, little ones—he grew deaf, and could not even hear his own music; can you imagine not even hearing your own little ones—how sad; but this did not stop Beethoven, no indeed—perhaps," he said, rubbing his chin and looking upward, "as he created his divine music, he merely laid his head upon his piano to hear the vibration of the keys—is it possible, do you think? Well, before I tell you more about him, I will relate to you a most tragic story," and as his tone grew sad, the Terns grew quieter, and as he leaned closer to them, they too moved closer to him; and then he whispered, with great passion and pathos, "When he finished conducting his *Ninth Symphony* for the first time, he stood, facing his orchestra; and do you know what happened next, my friends, do you?" He bent down even further, and they moved in even closer. "Promise not to weep, but one of his singers—I believe she was a contralto—came up to him and turned him round, and do you know what he saw," he barely murmured now, and all around him was absolutely still and silent, "he saw an audience wild with enthusiasm, standing and applauding, who knew they had just heard the first performance of one of the greatest symphony compositions in history—perhaps the greatest of all time." He wept, and as he did so, the Terns were absolutely still and quiet, and came to rest on his person and closer around him, as if he were sitting in a nest of birds.

"Thank you, good and kind friends," he finally said, wiping his moist, brown eyes, "but now," he said with enthusiasm, bringing light again into his tone, "let us learn and play—drum roll, please," he laughed, and tapping quickly upon his thighs, "no surprise here—the *Symphony No. 9 in D Minor, Opus 125*!" And presently, he was standing, acting as conductor and musician, and leading his obedient students in this sublime choral symphony.

After he and they, through his skilled maneuvering of their squawking chorus and flying movements, performed "Dance of the Hours," Act III, the finale, a ballet from Amilcare Ponchielli's opera *La Gioconda*, and *Carnival of the Animals*, by Camille Saint-Saëns, he excused them for recess, watched with joy as they flew around the sanctuary, and ate to their heart's content.

So, when the day was done, and his little friends were done, too, he would lie flat on his back and admire the glittering stars, and then address his beloved. "Adele, this all seemed so impossible, and now it seems so easy, too easy, but I wonder, Adele, might any man have made it? How many men would have walked off this isle and gone home and forgotten?" He looked at the cameras. "What information have you collected? Will you have psych evaluations ready for me? How can you know what I went through, how do you know that you wouldn't have done this too, that this was the right way, at least for me, to survive? O Adele, the sufferings of prisoners of war—at least I have in you my family, there, and in the Terns, my family, here," and he nearly wept, "to separate Man from his own kind, from all living things—is this not a true oblivion?" He felt as if she were here with him now, as if he expected her to respond to him, now.

\* \* \* \* \*

It was February now—he knew this by the position of the stars—and he was anxious to return home. He was resting peacefully on a cold and clear night when he awoke with a start. The Terns were gone. He looked round and saw a figure who was dressed in black sweats and a black hat and black sunglasses and a black mask standing next to the curved walls. Stuart leaped up, his body trembling with horror; he wanted to speak but he refrained. "Are they here to test me? Is there something wrong with Adele? Baby, is there something wrong with you?" he thought.

The unknown visitor continued to stare at Stuart, and then moved aside and a projector could be clearly seen. The visitor turned it on and stepped aside. The images appeared on the walls. It was Adele.

Stuart smiled largely and felt a joy he thought he had lost, but then he turned away, thinking that such images would ruin the experiment. "I can last a few more months; why are they doing this to me, to tempt me even now, how can they be so cruel?"

He could plainly hear the contents of this 35 mm film. It was Adele's sweet voice. He suddenly felt embarrassed and ashamed to be on the isle, to have done what he had done, as if he had lost his bearings in order to survive. He covered his ears but he could still hear her sweet voice, and she was laughing and giggling. "How can she be so happy without me?"

"Oh, I haven't been this happy in months…"

"What? What is this, what is she saying? Yes, she can be happy without me—yes, she can, what are these people doing to me? More of their games—yes, that is it, the fiends!"

"Oh, Jeff, I love you so much," he heard her plainly say, "and together we will have to tell Stuart that it is all over."

He felt a shudder through his body and his knees buckled. "It is not real, it is not; it is an actress who looks like her and sounds like her; they are trying to tempt me, like they do to prisoners of war."

But the same scene played on and he squatted down now with hands over his ears but he felt himself begin to stand up and soon he was looking at the screen and presently he was allowing his hands to drop to his sides; yes, it was undoubtedly her, his darling Adele, with another man, kissing another man, holding another man, making promises of love and fidelity with him. "It is a psychological ploy to break me, it is a trick, it is not real—I cannot believe Adele went along with it, but they must have told her it was part of the experiment," he thought, not wanting to speak to the voiceless intruder who stood with arms crossed and an empty countenance next to the projector. He picked up a handful of dirt and threw it toward the screen and then offered a rude gesture that would ensure that the enigmatic interloper would understand how he, Stuart, received this private screening. Presently, the masked person took the projector and disappeared through an opening in the wall. "There," Stuart shouted, "I have repulsed thee, villain!" And he laughed. "Even the birds know all about you, you miserable wretch!" He laughed again and began to violently move about. "They are messing with my mind, they are," he shouted, screwing up his eyes as he looked down at the recently returned and now trembling Terns, "they seek to get me off Bird Island with their subterfuge; it is just like them—the government—to do such a nefarious thing; they broke the rules, but I will not; they are liars, and I, a truth-teller; but I am disappointed that you fell for their lies, Adele." He shook his head. "The girl I know would not have played along with them, but we can talk about that when I get back and we decide how to spend their one hundred thousand beautiful dollars." He rubbed his hands together as he smiled greedily. "They don't want to lose their money, but I have news for them, Adele, I am going to take it and laugh long and hard and loud when I do, because we signed a contract and that is that." He thought of days gone by when the government broke treaties and promises to individuals and groups. "Just let them try and break this contract…" He went back to sleep and ate all of his food and enjoyed the next day and often spoke to Adele and the Terns about his plans for the future. That night, he went to bed confident that he had repulsed his foes.

He was awoken once more out of a deep sleep and when he looked up, he realized it was still very dark. The figure in black had returned. The projector was playing its lethal song. Stuart stood up and saw that his Terns were gone. He looked at the images on the wall.

Adele was engaged in an act hitherto unknown to any other man in the world except for her husband, an act not to be believed by Stuart had it been told to him or written to him, but now it was plastered in salacious black and white right there for him to plainly see, yet still he would not believe it, nor could he avert his gaze. And still he was voiceless.

The person in black stood with folded arms next to the projector, and neither smiled nor scowled, spoke nor laughed, and did nothing but occupy the space like a mute gargoyle; presently, the venom having been injected into the subject, the figure grasped the projector and disappeared through a hole in the wall.

Stuart cursed so loudly that the ducks on the other isles flew up in panic. "It's a dirty lie, Adele would never do that, she would never do that to me, she would not! It's a double." He massaged his head with great force as he analyzed the film and saw every frame replayed in his mind. "It looked like her and her body, it did, I admit that, they did a good job—but it's just special effects, it is, they have gone way too far this time, right, Adele? Baby, do you know about this— I mean, you couldn't know about this, could you? You wouldn't go along with this farce, would you, darling? I know you and you would not! Tell me that you would not do that, my love; and where are you, these days, why don't you come and visit your man? Why? Break the rules like they have broken the rules and tell me what it is all about—and I won't break, I won't, baby, I will be loyal to you to the end, I will, I will…"

The next morning, one of the Terns was dead. It was Scarlett. "You should have gone away during Winter," he said, mournfully, picking the limp body and caressing it; "you should not have sacrificed yourself for a human being," and he looked toward the walls, "we are not worth it, we are mere animals, but not as noble even as you; no, we can't live without hurting each other and burying each other every day with our lies and want of—things." That day, two more of the Terns died. He attempted to compel the other Terns to flee, but they would not leave their human master. "How noble, how brave you are," he said to them that night, petting Catherine and Heathcliff as they strolled over his squat form; "you do not seek to be beyond what you are, and you are better off not having thoughts, for it is thoughts that supply Man with cruel intent." He would wait now for the esoteric figure and the projector, but there was no appearance that night; so, he stayed up the next night and waited for the person, but once more he remained alone. "They seek to destroy my mind through bashing my skull with uncertainty, by making me wait and wonder when again they will come with their magic show and what they will show me; they seek to break me as the enemy seeks to break our prisoners of war; but I will not break, but merely bend, for I do not believe their lies; Adele is mine, and I am hers, and this bond they cannot break." He had an epiphany. "What if—what if they told Adele that I have gone insane here, or that I have fled from here and they cannot find me; but no, that would not explain her compliance with them, it would not explain what she—no, she did not do those things, not her, not my Adele."

One week hence and he was awakened once more by the black-suited figure and the noise of the projector. There, on the dark walls, the image of Adele appeared, and her voice was sullen. "Stuart, I am making this film of my own free will; they told me that you have seen the film of me with my fiancé, and that you also saw a film of us doing certain private things…" She paused. He disappeared inside of his mind. "It is over for us, Stuart, I am so sorry, I really am; but sometimes things just happen. It is no one's fault. You went away and I was lonely and I met someone else and it is just over, it just is; it's no one's fault, really, don't blame yourself, no, don't, don't do that; it would have happened anyway and I guess it's good that it happened now even though I feel kind of rotten that it happened while you were away." She pursed her thin lips. "That is all I have to say, Stuart—well, when you're through out there you won't find me here because I have already moved out. So long." The sordid image faded away.

There was a large rock that he had managed to secure from the muddy depths of the pool and now he lifted it up and heaved it toward the figure and presently heard a satisfying thud on the bony skull. Stuart stood up fully erect and glared like a stalking lion. The masked person recovered and then retired behind the walls.

By the next morning, more of the Terns were dead. "Dead for what?" Stuart cried, pounding the soft earth as he wept over the bodies of his friends. "Dead for a dead experiment; dead for a dead man." He lay down next to the remaining Terns. "Do you not see what you must now do, that you must leave this place to save yourselves? It is what you do, you cannot deny your instinct, my little friends; you must not do this noble thing for a human being—we are a failed species; so, you must go before it is too late and find delicious warmth." He would pick up one after another and lift them into the air and release them, but they would merely flutter back to the ground.

In a month's time, there were few Terns still alive. There were ducks on the other isles and many ducks had attempted to come to his isle but he had always rebuffed them. "You are not wanted here; no one could love you, for you have no loyalty."

He was sitting down, staring at the pale dirt. "I should have left when I found out; I should have left and then my little friends would not have died and I would have begun to live again, but here I stay because I have loyalty and honor, because I signed a document and I gave my word that I would stay until I could no longer physically or mentally survive; but I am still here and I can survive and it is not about the money, it is about who I am and what I must do to continue to be me or I will suffer the rest of my life; this is the way life is—you do what you have to do because you know it is right and it doesn't matter what anyone else does along the way." He would not say her name nor think about her but he still dreamed of her. He no longer believed the entire episode with her was a ruse.

He was maimed now in mind and body, his spirit having been violently hoisted up and hung and strangled until its very life essence was drained, where it lay limp like a thing dead; he was a prisoner now of mind as well as body, unable to extricate himself from his physical surroundings or his mental surroundings to a sanctuary where he might allow his spirit to fully breathe and regenerate; and consequently, his mind and body became lethargic, where he would sit still for hours during the warm day and stare at the surrounding wooden walls and lie down for hours during the night and stare up into the black theater of frozen space that housed the white celestial gas giants. The Gull-Billed seemed to sense his spiritual drowning, and they would groom him, as they had for many months now, picking insects and bugs from his bird cloak and his uncovered skin, and he would do the same for them, and keeping them warm until the natural warmth of the season came back; these once-screeching birds were now his only family, proffering a soothing comfort to him as they walked amidst him as if he were indeed their mother and protector and they his only friends and confidants.

The returning Gull-Billed built more nests with their expert precision in the yellow grass on the nearby shore, and soon there were a few manila-colored, spotted eggs; soon there were babies born and the mother and father were feeding them and soon enough the babies were introduced to their proud human father. "Where have we gone wrong," Stuart said once, petting the infants as they walked over his prostrate form, "that even the birds of the air make a better home than we; O, human beings, would that thought flow from us to them, would it corrupt them, too?"

One clear Spring night, when the great vault of heaven unfurled its glittering white jewels, when the sweet fragrance of budding life glided in the cradle of gentle breezes, when the world was wrapped in a gauzy blanket of tranquility and the benevolence and glad tidings of Creation, the courier came through the opening in the wall and came to the shore and stared at the sleeping man for the longest time, and then sent the bounty of supplies sailing toward its destination; and when the motorized boat smacked into the isle, the courier still did not leave, but commenced to making low, sobbing noises, and presently removed her mask, unveiling a golden plume of thick hair that flowed down to her slender shoulders. She held up her head on high, and her comely visage was consumed by such a loving and endearing smile it seemed that she would never smile at anybody the same way again, and then she waved with a profound sadness to the man and turned slowly and vanished through the wall.

The day of his release finally came and when he awoke, the walls were coming down, and his colleagues and Dr. Wright, holding brightly colored balloons, were waiting for him. Stuart was standing among the newly arrived Gull-Billed Terns like a loyal guardian, his long, thick black beard flowing down to his chest, his long, thick black hair flowing down his back, and bidding them a tearful farewell; and his skin was dark, his body muscular and lean and still covered by feathers and mud.

"A job well done, Stuart," Dr. Wright shouted from the path that was fifty yards from the pond as a small boat sailed across the still water, "we have enough information to last us a lifetime." Cheers abounded from the other professors and scholars who had been involved in the experiment.

Stuart looked at the boat and then looked at the isle and the chirping Terns and he hesitated. The boatman gestured toward the boat. Stuart looked again to the Terns and then to the humans on the dirt path and he stood, silent, brooding, still as stone.

"What is it, Stuart, my boy?" Dr. Wright asked. "Is there something that you need?"

Stuart looked again to the humans and then to the Terns, and then stepped onto the boat and stood as it sailed back to the shore; and once there, he stepped upon the pebbled sand and closed his eyes as he dug his bare feet into the alien soil. Now, no one was saying anything.

When he did ascend the small embankment to the path, he did not take the hands of his colleagues but merely walked right past them and kept on walking despite their queries and remonstrations and insistent words; he kept on going and going until finally he was running, running, just running down the dirt path until finally he turned the corner and disappeared out of the sight of his audience forever.

-Finis-

# Footprints in the Grass

G rass practically owns the surface of the planet. There is almost no place where there isn't some variety of grass—grass on the long prairies, grass on the burning savannahs, grass on the frosty Artic; grass is food, be it rice, corn, or wheat; grass supplies lotions, oils, and grazing for animals; grass holds the soil together, and together it becomes a broom, a basket, or a rope bridge; and where there isn't indigenous grass, there Man plants it, tends it, fawns over it, thus increasing grass' dominance over the world.

When Man slew his ambition to be a forager and settled down to live in an agrarian society, he built himself a house from the inventory of Nature, and when he did this, he gazed out at the barren soil that stretched before him, and decided, in his growing wisdom, to adorn it with native grasses and flowers; but in the Modern Era, he decided to adorn it mostly with a great variety of grasses. It is here that we must now examine this curious ritual.

A lawn is often the reflection of the people who live in the house it fronts. Grass is a point of contention amongst neighbors, it is a boon or bust, it excites joy or rage, it arranges the mindset of visitors, it signs sensibility or recklessness; this creeping, cunning monolith is a mirror of those who have planted it and have killed pests for it and have fertilized it and wasted inordinate amounts of precious aqua pura on it. Grass is selfish, grass is vain, grass is merciless, and Man obliges it as if it were a living pet; and in some very special cases, there are those who have decided that a lawn, a very carefully manicured and kept lawn, has a very special meaning beyond its slender, verdant blades.

There are lovers of these precocious lawns who seem to occupy every neighborhood, sometimes around the corner, sometimes on the next street, sometimes in your very own house, but this time he will live directly across from you, and you will come to know him and his faithful green companion intimately.

This particular man lived in obscurity in the world of people, for he had no family, no friends, no job, as his lawn of Kentucky Bluegrass was his family, his friend, his job. He had found his talent in this world, and it lay in the care and shaping of a lawn. The man and grass bonded like man and woman, like a boy and his dog, like a beautiful woman and a handsome man silhouetted against a clear and warm summer pastoral sky.

He addressed his grass as Darling, and when in the morning he greeted its rich green hue, he was like any other jealous suitor—he was wont to compare his ladylove to the other females in the neighborhood. "Bah," he often said, stroking his salt-and-pepper beard as he inspected the other lawns that spread before him, "disgraceful and shabby; they should all be plowed under, the whole lot of them." Yet it must be stated that if he had seen a lawn even approaching the imperial dignity of his Kentucky Lady, he would have wanted it destroyed, too.

When that hunk of gray rock in space was fat and the black sky lean, and silvery beams were sprinkled across his lawn like luminous, shiny pearls, he would sit down in the center of his lawn and smell the fresh life of it and dig his bare feet into the very heart of it, and finger its individual blades and imagine them his very own offspring; he imagined it as a singular honor for one of the grasses if they were to be plucked and examined by his expert eyes; and so, sometimes he would follow the thin blade down the stem with his slender finger and feel the nodes down to the roots and then dig deeper and tenderly grab and pull upward. "This won't hurt a bit, mon ami," he would coo; he would hold up the naked plant and inspect it for fungus or browning, or any sign of disease. "Ack," he would sometimes cry, upon beholding any damage at all, and he would cast said grass into his ready shoebox, "have you infected your brothers and sisters, eh, you little rascal?" He would then put more blades next to the ones already removed for careful inspection, quitting only when he was certain that the blight had been circumscribed.

In the morning, he was wont to check the overall height of his little darlings. "Long ago," he would say to his tender beauties, as he knelt down at the corner's edge, laser level in hand, "I used an ordinary tape measure—how barbaric! But one must change with the times," and he would check the readings of the leveler at every corner of the lawn. "Ack, what's this, then? Some of you are growing taller than the rest? How is this possible, my little children? I feed you the same food, in the same precious amounts, at the same time, in the same prescribed manner; tsk, tsk," he would add, obviously pleased to scold his mischievous brood, and would bend down to the blushing offenders and clip their tops. "We mustn't be greedy with meals; if you receive too much nourishment, make sure your brothers and sisters have enough; share, you rascals!" and he would recheck the instrument after this routine to satisfy his expectations. "How can one have a prizewinning Kentucky Bluegrass lawn if it isn't even level from stem to stern—it just isn't sociable, I tell you!"

Indeed, his lawn had been awarded numerous prizes by various home and garden associations, organizations whose sole purpose, it seemed, was to award prestigious prizes to home-owners for maintaining certain sections of their residence in a manner altogether superior to their numerous and shy neighbors.

He often talked to himself, which was a natural course, as there was no one else about his place; now, there were times that he would think of clever things to say in the event any guests ever came to visit him; and so, when he was unable to improve the structure and integrity and aesthetic value of his house and garden, he would read proverbs and maxims and attempt to create his own wise sayings. He would role-play: "But madam, your face is only half-painted," and she would say, "Better to show men how beautiful I can be, but how pret-ty I am naturally," to which the wise man replied, "But madam, you have succeeded only in showing, by comparing the two sides, how ugly you really are." But, as he was an equal oppor-tunity offender, thusly: "But sir, you have offered only a partial summary of *Plato's Republic*," and he would reply, "Better to show women how smart I am, knowing more than most," to which the wise man replied, "But sir, you have succeeded in showing, by comparing two such scenarios, how ignorant you are." And so, by engaging in such mental exercises, along with reading copious and diverse kinds of literature, and selecting and listening to what he deemed the most pleasing music of his generation, he was able to quiet the natural ebb of loneli-ness and cauterize the wounds of his past.

When he was not tending to his lawn, he was refining the least little blemishes to near perfection on his white stucco, and eggshell-colored wood trim, the large, double-pane windows, the cherry-red brick wall, the rose bushes along his walls, the magnificent fern tree, the white clusters of Birdcage Evening Primrose; in the backyard, he had a large vegetable and fruit garden on either side and in the middle he had St. Augustine grass, which he loved nearly as well as the Kentucky Bluegrass, not because of its appearance, but because it did not seem as needy to him. "What good is a grass if it styles itself?" he often spoke aloud, and then said to it at such times, "But you should not be jealous of your cousins in the front yard; they are more fragile than you, and are not as even-tempered as thee—well, well, what would the world be like if everything tasted like vanilla?"

In the morning he often fixed himself a cup of green tea that was sufficiently infused with locally grown wild honey, and a small, crisp salad and two pieces of wholewheat toast with small pats of butter and dabs of sweet marmalade jam, and then eagerly joined his awaiting treasure outside. "Oh, what is this?" he would sometimes say as he inspected the blades with his measuring tape. "A shallow root has no future here; we water twice a week, and the little fingers dig deep." The sides of the blades were constantly trimmed to a uniform pattern, weeds dug out by hand, and natural fertilizer and seeds spread out in carefully measured handfuls as he crawled over his spongy kingdom.

One night he came out and surveyed the front lawn and gasped. "Egad, dog droppings!" He felt himself nearly faint as he came upon the malodorous glob of societal dung. "And urine, too, O great killer of lawns, pestilence from the second ring of hell! Better the plague than this! Ack! Death to strays—no, death to dogs that stray onto any lawn and dese-crate it with their poor manners!" He treated the infected sec-tion as if it were a toxic dump site, and was careful to remove every particle of waste. He reasoned that this incident was a result of a neighbor having recently moved in a few houses away, their snow-white husky in tow. "This is why men have wars," he declared, espying the house down the lane; "tres-passing on another man's property is a call to action."

Lester Federman did not procrastinate as other men do, he simply responded to things, and within a day, he had found a stinking crimson powder that would supposedly repel dogs, but declared, "Purple power on my beloved lawn—bah!" and found dog traps that were too small, and electronic stakes that promised to deter any dog, and so he cried, "What, soil the neighbor's lawn? Never!" The County Agency could not act unless the dog was actually seen by them depositing its scurri-lous chunks of rot on his lawn. "So, if I videotape a man com-mitting a crime, he goes to jail; yet, if I record a dog that has been released by its master to vandalize my precious beauties, that mutt walks away free, with its tail in the air—outrageous!"

Before he investigated it, he knew what he had to do. "A fence," he said to his Kentucky Bluegrass, "will keep out those poop terrorists." He measured the exact dimensions of the yard, bought the lumber, came home, and then realized he could not do it. "What good is beauty if it cannot be seen? Ack! I am a prisoner!" He retired to the safe anonymity of his house.

"A gun! No, I can't enjoy my home from jail, as much as I believe the dog needs to die for his unrepentant sins; well, a pellet gun? Hmm, no, perhaps as a last resort, but too dangerous with children about..." He checked the lawn again through his dark living room window, and saw nothing suspicious. "Moby Dick must have a regular poop schedule," he mused. He secretly was glad about the dog, for it strengthened his resolve that people were basically no-good, selfish, petty bullies, and he was too terribly glad to have nothing to do with them.

The dog deposited his power lunches onto the vivid Kentucky Bluegrass every day for a week, giving Lester over to much grief. His heart ached as he sat near the contaminated areas and gazed with affection at his lawn. "Murdered by a conniving canine, where is the irony in that?" He wanted to collect the foul feces and deposit them upon the guilty party's porch. "Is it possible the wretch doesn't understand his dog is a treacherous trespasser? Bah! The idiot knows, but the idiot doesn't know that dogs don't belong in a house or even in a fenced-in backyard, any more than a pig belongs on the sofa watching the news—that is why the poor, dumb dogs are always trying to get away from their poor, dumb owners; O, if an Emperor I, the first decree would be that any person who willfully allows their dog to squat and drop his duty upon his neighbor's lawn, that person must then eat said feces—O, happy day!"

One morning he came out to check on his lawn, he saw a man stepping heavily upon the grass. "Him too," he thought.

"Oh, good morning," the young man with the handsome visage said, "I live down the road—Jim Preston is my name—and I just want to apologize for my dog..." He had a plastic bag in his big hand and another over it, and he proceeded to pick up the offensive lumps of modern art. "We have been letting him out for a week—but it won't happen again." Soon, the task was done, but not by Lester's strict standards, as he would have to go in afterward, like a second clean-up crew, and finish the job; however, he was now somewhat appeased, shook the man's hand, and even though he desired to keep hot vengeance burning bright in his chest, he could not do it, and thus began to feel foolish that he had not approached his neighbor before.

The entire episode of the dog had redefined his love for the Kentucky Bluegrass. "How can I let anyone or anything trample upon my lovelies, even myself! Egad!" he shouted, clapping his hands to either side of his round face as if looking at his lawn for the first time. "Indentations everywhere! It looks like the surface of the moon! Well, we shall see about that!" And so, that night he thought and thought and thought, and when he needed a break, he ate some hearty vegetable soup, and then he thought again and again and again all through the night, and by rosy-colored dawn, he had dressed an idea born from his singular ambition. "Magnificent," he cried, as he drove to the local hardware store for lumber.

By the next night, after working nearly all day in the broiling sun, and by the illumination of his three one-hundred-watt halogen lamps at night, he had finished the project; and he stood there, hands on hips and admiring his handiwork. "By George, it is extraordinary—extraordinarily brilliant and original, yes sir; only someone like me would have thought of it." It was a protective covering, such as the kind of plastic cover people use to keep leaves and assorted debris out of their pool, but one made of two-by-four wooden pale yellow cedar planks. There were hundreds of such planks, and each of them set about one foot apart, the entire width and length of the lawn; at their ends, there was an attachment that lifted boards about a quarter of an inch above the grass blades. All of the wooden planks could be slid back and forth along the width of the lawn by a complex interlocking system.

He took his mechanical mower and with a large grin upon his wizened face, fed its two rubber wheels upon two parallel boards, and thus, he began to cut the grass without the wheels or his feet ever touching his precious grass. "Eureka!" he cried as he mowed, and once he was done, knelt carefully down on the planks to trim the few blades his professional lawn mower Series 100 had not, to his exact standards.

* * * * *

For those of us who do not regularly indulge in the exchange of the private song of our heart to another through physical contact, such a heart withers and becomes a lump of ice; and yet, if even one guileless creature—one who does not know better because she has not yet been captured by the meanness and corruptness of the world—proffers honest affection while expecting no reward of any kind in return, manages to breach our prickly, rough exterior and touch our sterile, stressed-out organ of first contact, our outer crust of bitterness and rancor will melt, revealing an inner being who has waited and begged and hoped for rescue since first we fell away from people and hid in the barren periphery of existence.

Glee formed a halo of dazzling smugness around his dancing body as he hopped from board to board.

"Hello," a small and timid voice interrupted his victory celebration, "my name is Hilary."

He looked over to the sidewalk and saw a young girl with long brown hair, who was wearing blue jeans, a pale shirt and an innocent smile. "Hello," he said, without thinking, and then wishing that he had not said anything.

"I am really sorry about Thor doing his business on your lawn; it's all my fault. I let him out."

"Thor, eh?" he said, his eyes screwed up in wonder, and then letting out a soft "humph," he considered the small creation before him; if there had been any animosity left in him against her father, it dissipated now. "Well," he said, walking off the planks toward her and thinking that it would be appropriate to smile so as to put her at ease, "don't cry over spilled milk, as my father used to say." But then he saw her frown. "Do you know what that means, young lady?"

"No sir, I'm afraid I'm too little to know stuff like that."

He joined her on the sidewalk, standing next to her while taking off his beige leather gloves. "And how old are you, missy?"

"Seven," she said, proudly. "I'll be in second grade when school starts."

"Seven, you say? Hmm, why, that is a good age, as I recall—a better age than any age when you're old," he said, and then rubbing his whiskered chin, continued on, "a time of frolicking and make-believe, if I am accurate." She knit her brows in bewilderment. "Fun, youngster, fun!"

She smiled. "I like having fun. Do you like having fun, Mr. Fanatic?"

"Eh, what's that? Mr. Fanatic, you say!"

"Yes, Mr. Fanatic, do you like having fun?"

"My name is certainly not Mr. Fanatic," he grumbled, thinking of the implications of it all. "It's Federman, Mr. Fed-er-man!"

"But," she weakly protested, "my mommy and daddy say the neighbors call you Mr. Fanatic."

"They do, eh?" he said, irritated, hands on hips now with gloves in hands and a mask of disdain drawn in mean stitches on his hot face. "Why?"

"Because you're obsesseted," she said, and pointing downward, "about your lawn."

"Oh," he cried, standing fully erect and fully defiant as he looked about the neighborhood of his veiled enemies.

"Mr. Federman, what is 'obsesseted'?"

"It's 'obsessed,' in the first place, and in the second place, it means worrying about something far much more than you should." His twitching face was still directed at the windows, where dangled curtains seemed to sway ever so slightly.

"But is it nice? I mean, is 'fanatic' nice?"

"No, no, they are not nice words, young one, I am not happy to report." His brown eyes were darting from house to house to detect even now the smallest movement through their glass eyes.

"It hurts people's feelings, Mr. Federman?"

"Yes, yes, it does," he murmured, as the cruel intent of the unkind label began to lay its wicked stinger into his thin skin, "and about me, me," he cried, pointing to his scrawny chest, "me, who never hurts anybody or bothers anybody; me, me, who minds his own business all the time, and who is now apparently the business of every busybody all the time—bah!"

Using her as-yet-undamaged superior sense of interpreting the slightest nuance in human tonal modulation, she grew sad, and then said, "Well, I am sorry if they hurt your feelings, Mr. Federman," and then, as only a child can, as only a person still trusting and full of love toward all of God's creatures does, she hugged him.

He, never having raised a child, was bereft of protocol for such occasions, and suddenly felt too openly human. He became frightened, for his dull life had just acquired a little dose of sunshine and its inherent brightness temporarily blinded him.

And then, after numerous honest conversations with his new friend, he decided to disregard the wooden planks. "Silly," he said, as he removed the embarrassed boards.

"Oh, how silly," she said, giggling.

After this day, she would come by in the morning on the way to her school, and he would greet her as "Miss Hilary" and say "Good morning to you," and she would curtsy, as he had taught her, and return his hearty salutation. He was there in the afternoon, working on his beloved Kentucky Bluegrass, when she would come running out of her house, homework in hand, eager for his help. Her parents watched anxiously from between the white metal blinds.

"Hello, Mr. Federman," Hilary cried one day, as she came skipping up to him on her jump rope, her brown ponytail bouncing, her smile bouncing too; and then sitting down on the white hot sidewalk, she said, "Tell me again about Freya."

"Did you forget already, little lady?" he said, smiling, and looking back from his kneeling position on the lawn.

"No, I just want to hear it again 'cause it's so interesting."

He came to his knees and rested his gloved hands on them. "Well, you see," he began, now pouring his hands over the celestial heavens, "when that pretty little Norse goddess would ride her chariot—drawn by..."

"Cats!" she cried, excitedly.

"Exactly, cats! Excellent memory, little miss," he said, looking at her again, and then once more he looked skyward, "and so, when she rose that golden chariot over the earth, wouldn't you know it, but morning dew," and here he wriggled his fingers and let them fall to the ground, "came raining down upon the earth to make the grass wet and give drink to the thirsty plants," and he looked at her with great anticipation, "and what else came down from behind her but..."

"Summer sunlight!"

"You're getting smarter every day!"

"Mr. Federman, tell me more about the gods, please!"

He did, he told her all about the Norse gods and how they lived happily in Asgard and how they came to have so many exciting adventures.

"Wow," she said, with her wide open eyes, which were as blue as the bluest cornflower.

"But I will tell you something about this Friday, little miss—it's just about the most important Friday of my life, that's all."

"Why?"

"Why? Why, the Best Gardens people are coming to take photographs of my award-winning Kentucky Bluegrass, that's all, my little munchkin!"

"Gosh!" she said, "but I thought photo-graphy people already came and took pictures—and what is a munchcan?"

"Photographers," he said, carefully, mouthing the words as she, by now knowing this cue when he wanted her to correctly enunciate words she had mispronounced, repeated it slowly and carefully. "This magazine is national—do you know what that means? It means that these pictures will be seen all across the entire United States of America—and I will tell you what a 'munchkin' is," which he said very slowly and carefully, and then finished with, "another day."

"Gosh!" she said, and then, scrunching up her radiant face, mouthed the new word silently.

"Gosh, you bet," he returned, winking and snapping his fingers, and then standing proudly, "it'll just be the greatest day of my life."

She frowned, and said nothing.

He bent down next to her and said gently, "Say, I know that funny little frown," and playfully wiped the tip of her button nose. "Well, what is it?"

"But if you had children, wouldn't they be the greatest day?"

He was thunderstruck. "All right, little missy, who has been talking to you about me?"

"Well," she replied, in earnest, "no one." He was awe-struck again, as he considered her utterly incapable of lying to him and had decided there were no advantages for her to adopt subterfuge toward him as any adult naturally would. "I just thought that maybe having a girl would keep you company, and you could talk to her and watch her get married, and stuff."

He slowly shook his round head. "From the mouths of babes," he thought, and then said with a glint of sorrow as he sat next to her, "I was married once, a long time—a very, very long time ago…" He grew silent, wanting to undo the tragedies of the past.

"What was her name?"

"Margaret," he said, smiling affectionately, and then he said, so quickly that his heart would not long for the impossible, "but she died."

She hugged him. "Well, I am going to my friend Chelsea's house," she said, smiling.

"Maybe one day you will have a bicycle to ride to her house."

"Oh, no, we're too poor for that," she replied, and turned and skipped away down the street.

And as he watched her go, he thought about how she had so easily said how poor her family was, and that it had not even seemed to bother her. "To be a child again, all of us, and not worry so much about the troubles of tomorrow…"

Friday morning came and excitedly he woke up, spooned his warm minestrone soup into his starving belly, went outside, and stood on his porch, aghast. "Bicycle," dropped like incendiary bombs from his gaping mouth, "bicycle tracks," he stammered, walking onto his beloved green pasture, and he presently fell to his knees, letting his shaking hands move slowly across the snaking grooves, feeling the upturned roots and mashed blades and stems. "I'm ruined," he whispered, squeezing his eyes shut and letting his head sink to his chest.

Hilary was walking past now, and she noticed Mr. Federman in his agony, and the scars on the lawn, and she ran to him.

"Stop," he shouted, hearing her and then waving her away, and seeing her begin to cry, he shook his head. "No, no, Hilary, it's not you, I didn't mean you, I just don't want anyone else's footprints on this," and he compelled himself up and then over to his driveway, where he sat down in a dead slump.

She hugged him, then. "Who would do such a thing?" she said, weeping now.

"Monsters, monsters…"

He summoned the police but they were not interested in his minuscule plight, and he cancelled his Kentucky Bluegrass showing and brooded all the day inside his house; and then at night he got into his old Blue Rambler and sped to the local sports store to place an order for an item that would arrive at his home two weeks hence.

He now kept a vigil at the window at eventide, and during the night he wandered the streets looking for teenagers on bicycles, but nothing of consequence seemed to happen at night, and during the day, it seemed that every teenager rode a bicycle.

Then, it happened, two weeks hence.

A youth ran across the yard at approximately seven-thirty in the p.m. Lester left his warm perch and crashed through the open doors like a man in pursuit of murderers. "Get off my lawn, you lousy punk!" he cried. The youth turned around and laughed uproariously, as ripe and flaming youth always does when decayed and dwindling age threatens them. Lester stood, fury rippling throughout his small frame, and he ran to retrieve his toy and then took his position inside, waiting for his prey. The youth did come back, or course he did, to flaunt an emerging conflagration of energy that rose and swelled in him every day that led him on expeditions of discovery up and down every street and alley every night, but this time he was accompanied by a co-conspirator, both of them on bikes and, riding swiftly, cut across the Kentucky Bluegrass lawn. Lester came up behind the security screen door and held up his iron toy but could not consummate the deed. He cursed himself.

After a solid week of him not even coming out of his house, a solid week of hearing and watching the local neighborhood boys taunt him as they rode by, after seven days of intense waiting and allowing enmity to build up in his bloodstream, he was becoming unaware of himself.

It was morning when a knock came to his ears—he was slumped over, half-asleep, in his brown leather rocker with his heavy toy across his lap—and he raised the thing and nearly launched it on its maiden voyage toward the door when he caught a slight sound.

"Mr. Federman, Mr. Federman, it's Hilary," the sweet voice sang.

His face blanched. "My God, my God, forgive me," he mumbled, shaking as he fell to his knees, perspiring profusely. He set the metallic instrument aside.

"Mr. Federman, are you all right?" she asked, as he opened the door, but he merely hugged her, weeping.

Together, they toured his ravaged lawn from the hot white sidewalk and cement driveway.

"Why are boys so mean?" she asked, looked at the chewed-up grass.

"I don't know," he whispered, "I suppose it's just who they are."

They sat down on the curb together.

"Mr. Federman, my mommy and daddy said that those boys are so mean because they know you care so much about your lawn."

"Yes, I suppose so," he said, wiping away the sweat of relief from his forehead, "but a man has to care about something, and guard it; it's not bad to protect the things you earned and care about, is it, Hilary?"

"I suppose so," she answered; "my mommy and daddy protect me."

"You're a lucky little girl," he said, looking at her with admiration upon his tired visage.

"Well, I want to tell you a secret," and she leaned over and, cupping her hand, whispered into his ear, "my birthday is in eight days."

"Well, aren't we getting older," he said, smiling.

"And I want to you to come to my birthday party," she said, smiling.

The smile on his face fell as if it had been yanked hard by a sudden bad memory. "Well," he began, hesitatingly, "I don't know…"

In her voice of purity and love arose a small echo of profound disappointment. "But Mr. Federman, don't you want to come?"

"Well, yes, I do, Hilary, but, well…"

"You told me a long time ago that friends don't lie to each other."

"You're right," he said, still feeling her artless sentiment digging into his crusty heart. "I'll tell you what it is, it's just that, well, people around here don't really like me very much, and to tell you the truth, I'm kind of uncomfortable around most people."

She laughed very heartily at this as he stared at her in utter astonishment. "Oh, Mr. Federman, my birthday party is going to be at my house, and you are my friend!"

It was that simple for her, for she was still at an age when skin color or age or society status or religion or creed could not affect her decisions about the world as she knew it.

As it was, he gave her a tentative decision, and to that she was amenable, as hope and possibilities always mean victory to the young, as they always believe that one has only to wish honestly and passionately for something to make it transpire.

But then the ebony mists of night descended upon him and dressed him in its sticky molecules of gall and bitterness and stroked his rancor and increased his ambition for vengeance, and when two of the gleeful vandals cut across his beloved lawn, his tolerance for their youthful high spirits as a plea for clemency turned to smoke and ashes.

The next night, he sat at the window, his resolve being strengthened by the torment inflicted upon him by his relentless enemies and by his impotence to act according to the universal law which states that a man must protect his private property at all costs. He waited for hours, waiting patiently like a snake who waits outside the hole of the unsuspecting mouse, waiting to strike without fear or conscience; he would sometimes fall asleep, and then small echoes of noise would awaken him and he would rush to the window only to see the tiny monsters stopping to laugh at him and mock him and then scurry away. He did finally fall asleep and when he awoke in the morning he found his lawn mauled by scores of tire tracks—tracks that looped and skidded, tracks that tore deep and long like a dagger, tracks that spun horrific designs and ditches—and he vowed to destroy these creatures he now considered worthy of the most extreme punishment.

The next night came, but they did not come, and he fell asleep once more at the window, and once more cursed his weakness; the next night arrived and still they did not come, and once again he fell asleep on guard, and once again he cursed his weakness. On the fifth night of this vigil, at the zenith of his self-imposed sleep deprivation, when his mind had finally separated from his heart and soul, and he was seeing colors and images and ideas hitherto unknown to him, there came a whirring, giggling noise, and he was on the ready. "Minute Man," he mumbled, and opened the door in his waxen delirium.

And upon opening the door, he raised his shiny new toy, his twenty-gauge shotgun, and pointed both barrels at his menacing prey. "Die, now, villains," the human panther murmured, and his wretched heart pulled the trigger twice to deliver both barrels at his fleeing human rabbits.

Nothing came.

There was no grand explosion of satisfying sound, no powerful recoil from expended energy radiating through the butt of the wooden stock to his sagging shoulders, no youth flying high and cleft in twain and screaming in bloody pain as he skidded along the black asphalt and came to rest in his own vandal's blood.

No, there was none of it.

His face was ashen white as his mind dangled from the precipice of madness. He fell backward, stumbled into his open front door, tossed the rifle to the ground and dropped to his wobbly knees, his body convulsing, terror seizing him. "What have I done? What have I done?" he cried, and then burying his shameful face into his open hands, he said, weeping now, "What have I done, O Lord, what have I become?"

It was a nightmare he had escaped from, but he felt trapped in another, as if he knew this would happen again and he would not be able to prevent it.

And then he remembered.

"Yes, O yes!" he shouted, leaping up. "I remember now! I took out the shells after she came to the door; O, happy day that was, O, the little sweetheart; O God, she saved my life!" He looked upward and then bowed his head, his words solemn and planted in contrition. "O Lord, heal me!" and then fell to his knees. "And shield their eyes from what I so unjustly did."

Friday arrived, and there was much celebration at Hilary's house, there was cake and ice cream, Mom and Dad, pin-the-tail-on-the-donkey, Chelsea, friends and the cousins, and drop-the-clothes-pin-through-the-bottle.

"But where is Mr. Federman?" Hilary asked her mother.

"I don't know, dear."

A phone call came, and Hilary's father answered it. A minute later, and he called everyone to attention. "A surprise," he exclaimed, "everyone go outside!"

All of them anxiously walked down the street, Hilary holding her mother's hand, her eyes shut as instructed by her parents.

"Here we are!" Hilary's father shouted.

Hilary opened her crystal-blue eyes, and what did she see?

Mr. Federman was standing on his driveway, smiling like a proud father.

"Happy birthday, Miss Hilary," he sang, gesturing to the Kentucky Bluegrass he had literally sewn back together the past two days and nights; and all around the lawn there were colorful metal poles that had colorful string and glittering shells and multicolored flashing lights atop them; but in the middle of the giant lawn sat the grandest prize of all, and adorned with a big, big, pink ribbon with a red bow on top.

"A new bicycle!" Hilary exclaimed, but as she began to move toward it, she halted.

"What is it, Hilary?" Mr. Federman asked, in alarm, as he approached her.

"I have never," she said, shaking her head, "been on your award-winning Kentucky Bluegrass before; gosh, it's so beautiful."

"Oh, Hilary," he said, bending down and hugging her, "what good is beauty if you cannot enjoy it! Go now, go, young lady," he whispered, and then looking toward the glittering new bicycle, "it's all yours!"

He watched her as she slowly took her first steps onto the silky-smooth lawn, and with every step, as she approached the prize, her face was illuminated with awe and wonder;

and as she finally held the cool steel-blue handlebars in her small hands, she sighed in disbelief; and then turning to Mr. Federman, she said, pious tears in her eyes, "Thank you."

The last vestiges of ice that had clung to the heart of Lester at last dissolved.

But the celebration on the lawn was only the beginning, for just then, around the corner and coming with great theatrical thunder and music, came the circus: a real pony and a real clown and gobs of sugary cotton candy and a giant enclosed trampoline, and all of it right there and then came to rest on his precious lawn.

"Oh, I'm the luckiest girl in the whole world!" Hilary sang, hugging her mother and father, and then she ran to Mr. Federman and hugged him. "Do I deserve all this, Mr. Federman? I don't want to be like those spoiled children you have told me about—I want to be... humble!"

He hugged her back.

Mr. Federman, watching the children dancing and somersaulting and skipping about on his lawn, watching the children jumping on the trampoline and the clown juggling and the adults smiling and laughing, and the teenage bike riders who circumspectly glided in and then stood respectfully next to the joyous throng, felt that he had begun to slip back into something he had somehow fallen out of a long time ago; and then he looked at a small trail of impressions leading up to where the bicycle had once stood.

These were her small footprints on the grass.

Now he knew he was back in the human fold. "Yes," he said, and he laughed, and joined in the celebration on his award-winning Kentucky Bluegrass lawn.

-Finis-

# The Island of Him

No seed sown seeks the darkness
No seed grown seeks to wither;
No withered life passes a seed
A failed life dies alone

When he was a child he felt the boundless surge of youth flaring like a volcano within his healthy body, driving him, like a fire creates wind, to play and embrace the joys and wonders of existence; O, how he experienced the limitless marvels of life—of an indefatigable force within him gaining strength and power every sleep-filled, rejuvenating night; of his every breath bringing joy and happiness every joy-filled, adventurous day; O, how he worshipped at the sacred altar of all things fresh and new that made him feel invincible and incorruptible—of his budding life that was new, and his strong young body that was fresh, and his wondrously, lustrous dark brown hair and his smooth clear skin; and he was a child like any other child, full of love for everybody and every creature, wanting to be everyone's friend and every creature's master, desirous to please his mother and father, older brother and sister, and seeking the company of friends his age; all these things he desired because he felt an inner compulsion to do, to be around his own kind and to know them and, by doing so, to discover himself.

He filled himself up with the ceaseless energies of life every day, never knowing deterioration or stagnation, for his body was oblivious to rust and ruin, a body bathed in the divine light of immortality, a body building from raw materials that reached ever skyward, ever toward the nourishing yellow sun—this is youth, the youth that swallows everything dying and decaying in its path, youth that thrives on growing stronger every day and going faster every night and fearing nothing and knowing that deep, deep down it will never, ever die.

He was healthy as any boy, always eating and moving about: smiling and jumping and laughing and running, and running and jumping, and climbing and crawling, and always curious about the world and wanting to learn and to succeed and make his family proud of him; he was a handsome boy, too, and he adored girls, and although he was far too shy to resolve this feeling with them, it did not seem to matter, for he instinctively knew that he was still young and that there was still time, much, much time to decide such delicate matters.

Youth was a startling burst of ebullient fires in which he dwelled and worshipped and nourished, a magic elixir in a packet of concentrated energy, fantastic fuel that burned brightly and powered his movements and thoughts, a robust, mighty seed that would surely and swiftly grow and allow him to run faster and jump higher and run longer and jump farther with every moment.

But never could he conceive that this magnificent force would increase until it exploded and consumed the seed, wherein the host would return to dust.

His physical passions soared and he sought worlds to conquer—so he conquered sports, he did, he was a master athlete; and he conquered academic studies, he did, he was an intelligent student; but he still could not conquer that elusive creature, female—no, he did not, for he was still too awestruck by their beauty and charm and elegance, and their alluring yet alien character.

One day he chanced to look into a magazine and saw two pictures side by side of the same person—one that was very ancient, of a healthy lad standing proudly in his green Boy Scout uniform, and the newest picture, now much older, but who was now fat and balding and having gray hair and a sagging chin, the great conflagration of his grand youth having been extinguished long ago. The boy had a sudden revelation that he, despite his mere age of fifteen, would one day be like this old man, but also sad and lonely, isolated, unloved and forgotten—yet he could not properly interpret such a gloomy augury, and so let it go.

He worshipped the very idea of woman, his mind and body told him he must; he knew he needed their love, their intimate touch and calming spirit upon him as much as he needed the warm sun upon his cold flesh and a cool wind upon his warm body, a love he needed as much as bread and water, the sweet air he breathed, the cerulean sky he gazed upon—for to him, this love was simply a part of Nature that he needed in order to fully survive; he loved every curve and color of woman, every laugh and smile, every word and deed; he was intoxicated with their honey-sweet fragrance and their every move and action, for his body and his mind told him he must; he knew he needed them, had to have their delicate, small form next to him—he intrinsically knew all of these things, but never could he speak to them without trepidation and a befuddled mind spearing his equanimity; and still, he knew, there was time, plenty of time for him to find that one special girl who would want that one special boy, and then the two of them would marry and create that one special family and secure offspring to continue their seed and thus perpetuate the species. It had to be done and it would be done, and he knew this, in time he knew he would find her, and she him, so he was not worried at all when upon graduation from high school, he was still alone.

By age twenty-one he had lost his natural proclivity to blush and shrink away from comely women, and recently had courted several rather spectacular-looking females, and thus knew he was on his way, as his mind and heart and body instructed him he was. He still stood in the raging orange flame of burgeoning youth, still stood in its lustful soul, felt its eternal essence, and with it he was one, one with its divine nature and one in agreement, youth that willingly embraced the petty problems of the world and overcame and whittled them from a decipherable mass into a new kingdom to rule therein—and this he and his soon-to-be princess bride would do—it was only right and proper, it was owed to them, he reasoned, and it was so beautiful and free and natural that he could not understand how there was so much pain and horror in the world. He was not to be stopped.

And then it came, and he was unmade; he was forced down from the illustrious marble hall wherein dwelled the commanding spirit of youth and fire; he walked backward from its golden aura, his arms outstretched toward it, bewilderment etched like deep scars trailing down his burning cheeks, and he felt power and strength ebb within him far too early; and he saw his youth drain away from him like clear smoke through his grasping, jaundiced fingers; yes, the creeper, the destroyer, the conqueror worm had come—and its wicked form is scrawled in fresh blood on the fuming, crusty scrolls of history, and its terrible name is Disease.

He had ascended to the grandest heights to sit upon the highest throne when something wicked entered his magnificent form and crushed him to lay him upon crumbled stone; he looked around at the turning world and realized he no longer turned around with it; he looked at the world going forward and realized he was at an impasse; he looked at a world that was building and creating and prospering, and saw he was locked in a cellular prism of lethargy and weakness and suffering; and so, in a fleeting moment, the fabulous gains gathered from his youthful ambitions and labor were evanescent—his princess bride, his radiant health, his handsome looks; he had been lifted out of the robust season of life and dumped into the waning season of death, wherein old age creaked and cowered, molded and despaired, where he waited for the final dispatch to the celestial land of immortal souls.

His form was bedraggled and besmirched by Disease, his life juices squeezed and drained out of him; his body was bled and broken of its fullness and vigor; his hair was sparse, his face thin, his brown eyes dim, his mighty muscle dead; no longer would he continue to experience the great fount of energy that enabled him to run faster and jump higher and throw further; now, when he reached out his skinny hand toward the still bustling and hustling world of the living, they did not recognize him.

No doctor would or could help him, for any doctor who would was enslaved to his lord and master, mammon, and any doctor who could was enslaved to her ambition and career and yes, mammon, too, and had no use for curing this seemingly incurable patient; thus, he was dismissed by those who had taken a sacred vow to care for and heal the sick, just as a rich man, who by his very circumstance has taken a silent vow to bring succor to others in need, drives in his exorbitantly adorned car past a supplicating, homeless man, and does not recognize him.

He did not understand his illness but he tried, he really tried to figure it all out, but it was beyond his limited financial means and medical knowledge; thus, he was a prisoner of this morbid and ghoulish plastic surgeon, Disease, and all he could do now was try and survive.

And so he did live, as he thought he must, as a young man still must, but the charming ideas of youth had dissolved, the world of women had seen to that—they had conspired against him to strip him of any progeny, as they would tolerate no diffident and grotesque mate in their very private nest.

Women avoided him as if he were a stinking, hideous bug that had slithered into their exclusive domain. He sought them as his mind and heart and body commanded, commanding him to seek a wife now, as he knew he must, but they were not to be there for him, as he was already too far removed from their consciousness, which ached for authentically handsome and healthy and virile men, as they knew they must.

Still, he had other goals in life, goals beyond himself, that would perhaps ensure a legacy for himself; he had been a great baseball player in high school and college, and pro scouts had scouted him, but the illness had laid him flat; his strength depleted, his muscles shorn, his confidence drained; and still, he had other talents, where he considered he might gain some kind of legacy, and so he pursued a career as a painter and sculptor.

By the time he was thirty years of age, his friends had married and were completing the necessary tasks Nature had formulated in their brains, to wit: to go forth and multiply; and despite his scrawny appearance and women's aversion to him, he still dreamed of family and the friends and activities that would complete his life, therein.

But he did not know, could not possibly imagine that the entire matter of his life—from this point onward to his death—had been settled; he could not know how far removed from the hearty crop of fertile men he actually was, how much he had actually fallen from this view, how plain and ugly and dispensable he had actually become to young women around him. And just as no judge of horticulture selects the withered rose, no healthy woman selects the withered male as prize; yet, he could not lay down his innate desire to mate, it was too powerful to abandon—it would have been just as impossible for him to abandon food and drink; O, how he yearned to be in love again, for he still remembered the warm bliss it had covered him in—a memory like a hero's welcome—the sweet caress of a woman's gentle touch against him, the idea that any woman would abandon all others to devote her life to him, and the special language between two lovers that cooed and hummed a serene song in his soaring heart.

His flesh was growing cold. No woman wanted him and this hurt him and cut him deeply and one day a tiny flake of ice settled in the cut and did not melt; he wondered if he were becoming forgotten, and this seemed utterly impossible to imagine.

And had he not pursued women still, had he not asked many, many women out on dates and had he not been rudely, tactlessly, and bluntly told in a humiliatingly and negative fashion, No, which meant, as it was conveyed masterfully by these attacking females: no, never you, you ugly and feeble-looking half-man, half-corpse, for your manhood has dried up, and as you are no longer pleasing to gaze upon, you are no longer good for nothing.

For they had crafted a digging grave within their bosom in which they had buried him, and fashioned a headstone increasing in weight, that described him: non es.

Disease was his master now, keeping him from family affairs and the joyous houses of friends. He watched the world configure without his presence—the world, he knew, did not need his contribution to survive. He was fearful of truly becoming obsolete, that he must act now, right now to have a chance for happiness—for if he did not right now go through his open door and find a woman to love and marry, he could not go later, for every moment he wasted, what little charm he had left was dissipating much too fast—but he could not, restrained by the ugliness Disease had carved into his emaciated frame, which repelled any decent woman; and so he feared that he would never have their special touch, never have a family, never have children, and this murdered him, frustrating him beyond measure, as if a tomb was being built particle by particle inside him until he was more dead than alive.

When he was forty years old, his brother and sister and his friends had children who were now grown up and some of his older friends even had grandchildren, and yet he was still alone, a pathetic, haggard soul who was on the outside looking in and craving the dynamics of family life and dying for his place in society—to love and be loved and have children and watch them grow up and he grow old with his beautiful wife and then die content—but instead, he was still impaled in the same egregious spot that was ruled by rust and famine of the heart: stagnation. And when he turned to personal triumph to ease his disappointment, he found none, for even the paintings and sculptures he had so carefully crafted and nourished as if they were his very own children did not sell. It was in these darkest valleys, when every aspect of his life seemed hopeless and fated to failure, that he began to convince himself that he would never marry.

He now feared that he was inextricably, unavoidably, irrevocably lost.

And still he dreamed of hearth and home, as he could not so easily shut off or close this ardent request as if it were a mere valve or an open window; and so panic, like a sudden and overarching plague, developed within him when he first looked around and realized that the natural course where he, as a young man, and where this mystical and archetypal she, as a young woman, would marry and grow up together and learn together and raise their children together and still be young when their own children had left their protective nest was gone; now, he lamented, for even if he did find a woman who would have him, she would be old, like he, old in her ways and set in them, too, like he, and perhaps a woman even with her own children and a menacing husband who had been torn from her bloody side but was still lurking somewhere in her strong orbit—but worse, she would probably be sickly, like he, and despite his illness, he still imagined a healthy woman for himself—this disturbing scene was sufficient to dry up his desire for marriage over and over again.

He began to realize and accept the notion that he would live alone until his ignominious death; any death conducted in obscurity, he had decided, was ignominious, any death

occurring in remote places and not accompanied by griev-
ing family and friends was not only ignominious to him but
cowardly and worthy of no inclusion in the sacred annals of
recorded history.

Every year he observed the disrobing of his majestic
youth, the passing of his gorgeous youth beyond the mystical
curtain of history—one more empty year, one more misbegotten, meaningless, meandering year trodden upon by his
regret, sorrow and desperation; and yet, he could do nothing but assist his melancholy repose as he sank deeper into
the abyss of oblivion, for this malevolent, merciless ripper,
Disease, had seized him with her fanged forceps and raised
him up to dangle and tease him above the acrid pit of death.

He thus began to see the world crumble before him, its
basic structure altered and rebuilt by his growing despair. Soon,
he knew, very soon he would be alone—for his mother and
father had died, his friends and brother and sister had moved
away—and too often he contemplated this as he sat in his own
growing distemper and contemplated the raggedy black fog that
was encroaching upon his strained senses. He began to consider
total isolation, and as the very thought of it soothed his pain,
he allowed its cunning spirit to enter into him and tempt him.

The first time he sought to refrain from speaking to
friends and relations by unplugging the phone and not
answering the door, nor opening any letters from them, last-
ed a mere twenty-four hours. He cursed his own weakness,
knowing he must be ready for the day when he was truly
alone, and if at that time he yearned for human contact, and
none was readily available, he knew that madness would
surely destroy him. He had to gird himself for such a trial.

When he was forty-five years ancient, depression, black,
bountiful and bleak, crept in, weighing on him like a swarm

of leeches, sucking his ability to produce beyond the basic needs of work and personal care; yet, it also strengthened his resolve to block out the need for human companionship; when in years past he would rush home and call an acquaintance concerning an event of interest in the news or his desire to attend the cinema or go on a short trip, now he refrained, and let the urge to bond with his fellow humans die like a baby bird crawling and gasping for life in the miserable scorching heat of the desert; and he dreamed of marriage and babies, still—still he dreamed of beautiful weddings and his health returning and family and friends and life beginning again; and yet, as the macabre creeper of depression sifted into his very pores and displaced his will to live fully and happily, he began to have days where he spoke to no one—no one at all in any way, an act inconceivable only three years before—and where he began to have real days where he convinced himself that he would never be married.

Slowly then, surely then, he began to bow before the relentless, gnawing claws of depression and fall willingly into its iron sepulcher and nestle there and be content there—at least a place, this, where he knew what and where he was and the expectations of him and where the real truth of the world lay, and where no lie existed—here he was dead and buried and forgotten, and he expected nothing beyond it; and so depression became his deliverer from the uncertainties and failures of life, and in this shrine of sorrows it became his soothing mistress. Inside her pungent bosom, he was allowed the time to think about what he had become, and he knew what he finally was—alone.

Thus, it was here in the sweet caress of profound melancholy that his mind began to assimilate that which was hitherto unknown to his once-ebullient nature—a craving for solitude, and a despising sentiment against those whom he reckoned had sentenced him to be here.

And then the horrible bouts of sobbing commenced as he ruminated on his failed life. These hot tears were messengers that leaked through a fissure from the dense structures of his breaking heart, and every time a horde of these spherical droplets rolled down his sunken cheeks, it was as if he were losing a small piece of his humanity; and when the emotional tumult would abate and he would gain his equanimity, his crimson wrath would set in and he would sit in the darkness and rage against an uncaring world. He did not have to weep too long or too many times to realize his shame and humiliation, and then vow that he would never, ever weep again for anybody or anything for any reason. As his greatest desires had died, he too had died; as his greatest joys had died, he too had died; and as his greatest and most fervent dreams had died, he surely died a most horrible and excruciatingly slow, spiritual death.

This was the time that the repugnant idea of suicide first aspired for recognition within him, but the illimitable power of a youthful parade that would never conceive of such a transgression still had momentum within, so it could not yet take root, just as even the most virulent of weeds cannot take root amongst robust and dense plants; but it could also not take root because of what he read about people in his private and sacred books, those with horrible diseases and awful handicaps who somehow went on with life and even strived to do good for others—this too was enough to quash what he considered his whining sentiment.

Within two years, he could easily go one week without the need to speak to human beings—although there were still specks and shreds of a long-ago feeling that all of this was wrong; in three years' time, he reasoned, through daily talks, that he would never be married, a daily ritual he practiced, while dressed in anger and tears, in earnest and passion all the day and all the night; and still—still, his dreams betrayed his now-buried true self, as he dreamed of young beauties and himself a handsome young man, and love, too. But it was too late, he was undone.

By the time he was forty-eight years of age, his emotions had been encrusted in stone for a year, as he had by then lost all hope for love, lost all need for human contact, and begun actually to abhor women and everyone else because he felt they had betrayed him. Yea, his hard flesh had turned to hard stone—polished, clean, and barren, and cool and numb to the touch—for he had no physical contact from other human beings, no simple hand upon hand, no life-sustaining arms around another, no loving souls in an elegant and fleshly embrace that all people needed as much as precious food and water and sunshine; so, he stood, this great unfeeling monolith, needing no comfort from his own species, and he thought himself happy: because he had become his own wise counselor, his own amusing dinner guest, his own best friend, and all of it accomplished by being alone and talking incessantly to himself and to his great and silent and obedient companions, his most loyal allies—his books, his television shows, his movies—and with long stays in Nature, and melodic, gorgeous music to infuse a vibrant color and sparkling gaiety inside his emotionally starved heart and mind, his insular world was negotiable and sustainable. Every day he rushed home from his job, where he had very little human contact, to read exciting passages in his newest book, to eat delectable food in front of the delectable television shows, to listen to the majestic scores of classical music as he shut off the burdensome lights and allowed his mind to simply wander and feed upon itself. And so, in this manner, he achieved long stretches of isolation from his fellow creatures without seeking their company.

And still, the idea of a satisfyingly quick and painless suicide began to surface within him when he could not properly hold back the menacing tide of self-pity; so he began to muse upon the most expeditious methods, to wit: pills, bullets, or cliffs—razors were too messy and ropes were just plain barbaric. He decided that there should be a better variety than these if one dared to be the clay and the clay maker; and still—still he did not terminate his miserable life, and more of late it was because of the valiant people he read about who were just plain worse off than he could ever imagine but somehow, someway, in some impossible-to-imagine universe, struggled on and even contributed to society. This shamed him to live a little while longer.

Thus, when he retired, he had affixed himself a companion that would carry him to the end of his days—apathy toward the world; and when he did think about people he had known, he imagined them as being mute, thus ensuring that those from the past would stay buried in the past. He no longer cared about having a family—the families he saw sickened him because he saw only the flaws and blemishes therein; he no longer cared to have friends—friends to him were merely opportunists who exploited his resources; he no longer cared to participate in any ritual that needed a mass of humanity to engage in—he needed the world only for basic goods and services, and nothing else.

He had long since reasoned that he would never marry, but had not quite convinced himself of this, that he would never have the special magic and joy that a family

brings—magic like the magic of marriage, joy like the joy
of family; magic and joy of the firstborn, and the next born,
of baby's first step and words, and debut in school; the magic
and joy of graduation from high school, and then attend-
ing university; the magic and joy of a child's marriage, and
then grandchildren; and the magic and joy that never ceases
because he had closed the life loop—grandchildren growing
up and having more children and thus continuing the family
name. There is always magic and joy for the family man, he
reasoned, who by virtue of his union with his woman perpet-
uates the species, that every time they hold close their own
dear flesh and blood, the magic and joy never dies; but he
would never have this chance, and never experience the real
magic and joy in the sacred privilege and honor of creating
life where before none existed; for his only chance for any
kind of magic and joy, albeit temporal and shallow, where
he might have left something to survive him, his career as
a painter and sculptor, had failed, and failed miserably and
humiliatingly—for his paramour, Disease, was a jealous mistress, and determined that he be hers, and hers alone.

And he had long ago stopped weeping for anyone he
knew who had died, never even began a pious tear, not a
salty pearl-shaped drop, not even moisture in the eyes when
he went to the mirror to see the numb, dead expression of a
man who no longer fit in the world nor even cared to be in it.
This was, in and of itself, frightening to him, and he wished
he could weep for this dead shell of his strangled soul—but
alas, he could not; but soon, he was glad, because he did not
seek to weep alone.

So, now he was emotionally amputated from the living
world, adrift on a frozen sea of ice, too far from the shore
of green to ever smell its fragrant scent of hope and feel its

velvety texture again. And now, he began to muse longer on questions that had been his crucible from the very beginning: why am I suffering? Why am I alone? Why? Why me? Is there some benefit to this? How could I possibly be a better person because of this emotional desolation?

In five years' time, he had not answered the phone for five years, nor any letters, nor answered any invitations; now, he rarely left his humble home, and then only to shop for food and essential items needed for survival; ah, but he now knew he was truly happy. His secret desire was to leave civilization and live on a high mountain far away from the ravages of people: their intrusive nature, their duplicitous nature, their rude and vulgar nature toward all things unlike them that compelled them to want and crush it, but he had neither the finances nor the willpower to do so. And still, when he slept, he dreamed of women—young and beautiful women, and he as a young and handsome man, and he was together with them in the land of a surreal fantasy, and there he was truly happy.

He had long ago decided upon pills for suicide, reasoning that bullets were too messy, and cliffs too unsure, and he thought about it often, about its charming power to relieve every emotional and physical ailment from his body like some magic elixir, and he threatened to visit its undiscovered fields of illusions soon; but more often than not, it was still his reliable and endearing books that were full of stories of tragically ill and physically disabled people who just should have capitulated and died, should have begged for death, should never have done anything other than mercifully expire after their condition was known and the inexorability of time had a chance to increase its burden upon them and suffocate them like a boulder on a bug—but no, these terribly courageous individuals would not let their bodily dysfunction stop them from going forward and up and to where they sought to be, as if, yes, as if somehow they had not let that horrible something that happened to carve up only their body carve up their heart and soul and spirit, too; and so it was this: this too often, and this too much grown into his mind that if these people could persist beyond what he considered an unacceptable life, he could go on, too; and so he inevitably did, and let the surging wave of a coward's death wash back with the retreating tide of self-pity.

He had long ago put up "No Trespassing" signs upon his property. He did not talk to neighbors, and avoided them at all costs—he would retrieve the mail from the communal silver metal boxes when he was certain no one was there; he would get in his car only when he was certain no one was in the street outside their homes; he sometimes waited for hours until his street was void of human life.

By age sixty, he had not engaged a human being in a friendly conversation in five years. He hurried past any person he encountered on the outside, avoided their touch, his head always hung down low; he mumbled the fewest words necessary when he purchased goods and services and rarely looked at the attendants in the face; he cheered whenever he reached his car after shopping, for inside this rolling sanctuary there was security and safety from the awful Them.

And still he dreamed of what might have been, but awake, he knew it never had been and never could be, and now he did not want it to be. He wished he could sleep forever.

In one more year, he was having nearly all of his goods delivered to his house, and he had achieved near total seclusion from people; now, he never left his safe house except to retrieve the mail; now, he barely showered, hardly ever shaved, hardly changed clothes, as he was living to please himself, and anything he seemed to do pleased him.

Suicide was a constant thought as much as the thought of his life, for it had bored into his life like a parasite that sucked his resistance to die without good cause; and still, he somehow managed to assuage its ill-humor and keep its sharp sword sheathed because of those he considered true heroes beyond the understanding of healthy individuals and even people like himself, those who were sick or physically disabled, that somehow, someway had learned some real magic and joy in the world through their own suffering and ordeal—and how could someone who could not even approach their level of pain not desire to understand it?

The world changed, and he did not; it evolved and he crept about in his cozy lair; it moved on, and he dawdled and hummed, sang and read, laughed and danced, unaware and uncaring about anyone or anything. He no longer took the newspaper, for he no longer cared about the world; he no longer watched the news, for the only news he sought was of his own sad self; wars erupted and stopped, catastrophes occurred, plagues threatened, and he did not care about any of it; no, not one bit, because the world, he knew, was all about itself and not him—him it had abandoned, he knew, and so he had abandoned it; and his life-shearing Disease had adopted him and kept him close to its spongy, oily body, and therein he dwelled, inhaling the sooty vapors of his growing depression, and herein he lay, day after day, waiting for death, waiting for oblivion, praying for death, praying for deliverance as he sank deeper and deeper into his petty kingdom of isolation; and here he did not weep or lament, for he had climbed into the abyss of his own making, an abyss created by his own bitter will to hide in, to martyr himself in, to wallow in, where he alone ruled and was ruled, where he alone was prosecutor and defender, judge and jury, executioner and exonerator, a victim of genetic inheritance, a victim who denied the good in himself and the good in the world; so, here he became a worm in its own finely spun cocoon where he dreamed of becoming a beautiful butterfly.

And as he imagined death one day, as he lay there on his gray carpet with a graying body that was still as a petrified log, he reached out his arms and imagined himself a comely man with a comely woman and the both of them deliriously happy and in love; but now he wondered why, why him, what had happened to him, why had it all happened to him—the virulent Disease invading his healthy body, his life destroyed because of it, women abstaining from entering his sphere of influence long enough to appreciate his youth and person- ality, the shredding of his connection with the world, his long, slow, tortuous slide into anonymity; why, he wondered, hadn't someone rescued him, why hadn't some good soul— weren't there plenty of good souls who performed good deeds in the world—simply lifted him up and out of his repressive funk? Too late, he knew, too late to live again, all is lost, all is gone, all is dust and ashes, like a sand castle at the shore— we are young and strong, he reasoned, and then the forces of Nature, who built us and nourished us, then seeks to bring us down one grain at a time; yet had he not been an agent for his own destruction, he contemplated, did he have to cut himself away from the world, could he not have had, if not a family, at least friends? Must life be only about family? he wondered, lying there and staring up at the dull interior of his home. Was there something more to life than family; was there something more important that he had missed? Did the world demand that some will forfeit family, and for what purpose? Must he contribute to the world, and if so, how could he do so if he was bitter and alone—did he know invaluable things that others did not know? Did people of his kind go where others had never been and learn things others can never learn, only to return and be a benefactor, an ambassador to others—but whom? And why, why must some suffer? Of course, he had had these kinds of disturbing thoughts a thousand times before, but such contemplation had never benefited him in any way so he had always treated them like a importunate bacteria or virus that needed to be isolated and crushed and removed from his body and lain like a corpse on the outside of him so the inside of him could live its solitary existence inside its sulking chrysalis.

And so, thankfully, and finally, he died, because he knew it had been too long that anyone cared about him and knew no one ever would again.

At least, that was what he wanted, he wanted the para-medics to come and find an old, diseased body, mummified, perhaps propped in an old brown rocking chair in front of the buzzing television set. And who would care, he wondered, what was it all for—so a man does not achieve immortali-ty through his own children, and a shared identity through his own wife—is there not more to life? He dined on these thoughts as he lay there, and no physical food went into his body then, but spiritual food, and no physical water went into his body then, but spiritual water, and the spiritual food and spiritual water fed his eager mind for three days.

What was an epiphany to him now but a flowing out of the stagnant waters that contained nothing but the old ways and the refusal to consider what might be otherwise, and a flowing in of sparkling new waters that he had drunk from the present and past, but had refused its entry; revitalizing water that contained everything feared but now understood to be salvation and restoration, as this: he realized that he had spent nearly his entire adult life despairing about his own pathetic problems that, in the light of the history of the world, were meager and meaningless: had he not once a good job, money in the bank, food on the table, clothes on his back, a roof over his head, living in a Democracy in the greatest superpower in the history of Mankind, and had he not a life that was better than the greatest majority of people now living and who had ever lived? This uncontested truth hit him between the eyes like rocks thrown by every poor child round the world.

Had he, then, he mused, wasted his entire life despairing about what he had not accomplished, or did not have, or desired, and by doing so, accepted without question the wrong theme, to be his only saving grace? Must only his failures constitute his life—just because his personal desire had not been fulfilled, could he not help others reach theirs? Was he on earth just to help himself, he wondered, or by helping others receive help from others, and perhaps, just perhaps, find another kind of happiness he had never considered? Had he not read about the people in his books, who were in far worse physical conditions than he, and done the same? Still, why must he suffer—why him? And then the full weight of his poor life came crashing atop him. How much had he truly suffered, he thought: I am not in war, not in a hospital, not in prison; I have all of my senses, my limbs, I can move about, I do as I please; and where am I, if you please, is this Paradise, where there is no suffering or pain or tears? No! Here, we suffer, it is the way of things—people are fond of lamenting their fate here, as if there should be nothing but joy and love and happiness, but this is false, and so we must accept what is, and work to ameliorate the emotional sorrow of others, for only they know what true pathos and pain is, true heartache, true loneliness; and perhaps, just perhaps, he thought, as I help others less fortunate than I, someone would dare to even help me—but it is too grand an idea to even consider, and I am even ashamed to think I need help, for as I think of it now, the only one who created my problem was me, and it should never have existed, and should be forgotten; so, now, I am whole.

He was thunderstruck.

On the third night of the third day, his wrinkled face was stained with tears—he had not cried for so long—and his still body was dehydrated and hungry; and then he struggled to stand, and upon reaching the bathroom, stared into the mirror as if beholding his face for the first time. He retched.

He showered and shaved, found clothes long ago forgotten, dressed himself, and after a small meal, walked to the front door and opened it, and as he walked outside into the rejuvenating sunshine and stood on his porch, all human life about him came to an abrupt stop.

The adults on their lawns froze, the children playing in the street froze, even the dogs, sensing this eerie event, too froze—the cats did not freeze because they were not paying attention, nor could they ever be expected to; no neighbor here had ever seen in the daylight the one they called the old hermit, but now he just walked right down that sloping white driveway and boldly across the street to offer salutations to the youngsters and right up to the adults to shake their hands and introduce himself. For the next week, no one in this neighborhood seemed to talk about anything else except the story of the emergence of the old man who possessed a stunningly amiable character.

Presently, he was in his car, and he knew exactly where he was going because he used to drive by it many times and often wondered what life must be like inside it, and so there he went. He arrived at the Cedar Brook Retirement Home and went directly and confidently up to the clerk and declared that he wished to visit the residents therein, as it was, he said, the duty of those still physically able to visit and bring succor to those in need of it. He had a splendid day there, talking to many older men and women, hearing their life stories and having wonderful conversations with them; and when the day was nearly over, he walked over again to the clerk and asked her who the loneliest, most forgotten resident was, and the clerk immediately told him, but admonished him that this woman would accept no visitors. He smiled then, and said, as sagacious people often do, that it would all be just fine, and then took out a piece of paper and wrote something on it; and somehow, in the smooth cadence and tone of his words, she believed him, as if in his long years he had gained great secrets into human nature she did not yet know but hoped to understand.

He soon found and knocked upon the ugly green door of the small room of the reclusive woman, but she did not answer; but he was not deterred, and so he simply placed the paper under the door and departed.

He returned every day to the retirement home, and made many new friends there, but always, at the beginning of his stay, he knocked upon the door of the woman, and as he always received no response, he placed another piece of paper under it. For three months, he arrived early at the home and stayed late, but never did he receive an answer from the woman behind door number twenty-three.

It was Christmas Day now, and he came early in the morning, bearing many wonderful gifts, but first he came to her door, and once more placed a long piece of paper under it; and that night, when the residents were engaged in joyous song and wondrous stories downstairs, he once again walked up to her door and knocked upon it and announced himself.

Come in, she said.

His hands swept up to his face to contain his pooling of tears, and after he had composed himself, he entered. She was sitting in a wheelchair—gray-haired, small, frail—and on the plain, gray blanket in her lap lay all the papers he had slipped into her tiny universe. She asked him to sit down.

She had read them all, she said softly, her arthritic hands holding up the letters; she had read his entire life story and she was so very much like him, she whispered, fondly.

Won't you come downstairs and join in the festivities? he asked gently, and upon standing, stretched out his hands toward her.

She smiled sweetly, and asked him if this was a date. He too smiled and said that indeed, it was.

She consented and so he wheeled her out to the brown carpet and to the top of the special ramp and carefully moved her down it.

O, the excitement that echoed throughout the hall when the couple appeared before them; O, how the cheers, the applause, and the gathering round of people to greet her built a magnificent palace of love!

And then he said, smiling, joyfully, abundantly, "I would like to introduce you to a friend." Tears of piety poured down his flushed face.

The entire place became breathlessly quiet, as everyone there was looking at her with great affection and anticipation as she said, weeping, "I am Evelyn Keough, and I would very much like to get to know each and every one of you."

Life!

My restless heart thirsts for love
My tears, my bitter drink;
and now I have real love,
and joy, reigns in me

-Finis-

www.ingramcontent.com/pod-product-compliance
Lightning Source LLC
Chambersburg PA
CBHW020246150626
46552CB00020B/559